ADRIFT

VP Saxton

Library of Congress Control Number: 2018904365
ISBN: Hardcover   978-1-5434-0839-3
               Softcover   978-1-5434-0838-6
               eBook   978-1-5434-0837-9

Print information available on the last page.

Rev. date: 04/16/2018

To order additional copies of this book, contact:
Xlibris
1-800-455-039
www.Xlibris.com.au
Orders@Xlibris.com.au
771439

ADRIFT

CHAPTER 1

"You're moving," Carla said incredulously as she watched the burly estate agent hammer the large For Sale sign into the patchy front lawn. The photographs advertising the property looked appealing. Carla thought someone must have been busy photoshopping, as she hardly recognised the place.

"I know, Carlz. I'm really sorry I've not said anything before. I knew you'd be upset. But really, there isn't much choice." Helena's slightly bloodshot eyes appealed to her neighbour of almost twenty years for understanding. "Mum's gradually getting worse. You know that. And she needs almost full-time care now. It somehow seems unfair to make her move here."

"Of course, Helena. Sorry to be thoughtless. I guess I just always surmised your mum would move in here with you rather than the other way around. But she's got that big house. It makes sense." Carla laid a caring arm around Helena's shoulders and felt guilty as she watched tears slowly ebb from her friend's eyes. "I'll put the kettle on."

A small terrace of just three homes was built at the bottom end of a cul-de-sac when old Mr. Murray finally agreed to sell the last of his plots of land. Canny to the end, he reserved the site until the residences of Capstan Court were well established and the area considered desirable, knowing that three well-designed houses would command a relatively high price. A good deal of speculation went on as to what kind of development would occupy the vacant lot. It turned out to

1

be a pleasantly attractive trio of residences that deceived the eye into thinking one generously proportioned building filled the space. In reality, the double-storey central house had a garage on either side of the front entry. The living quarters extended backwards. It was edged on three sides by a narrow garden. At the back of the property, a small grassy area formed a lawn. A shed stood in one corner, allowing space next to it for a clothes hoist. On either side of the garages, copious bay windows allowed natural light to flow into the living rooms of the two remaining houses. Curved pathways led to each front entrance located around the sides of the structure. Driveways allowed their cars to be driven to garages at the rear. The red-brick finish afforded a rather grand air to the completed whole.

Carla and Douglas were the development's first occupants, taking the central house because it proffered an extra room. It was priced at the absolute maximum they could afford. The garden was smaller than the two outlying properties, but seeing as all three were priced equally, they decided to go for accommodation rather than potential flower beds. Lizzie and Mike had swiftly followed, clearly making their mark by unashamedly parking their bright red Jaguar on the driveway. It was a short while later that Helena and Greg had moved into number 26. As it transpired, they borrowed the deposit from Helena's mother. Greg had been rather concerned they would always be seen as the "poor relations" by comparison, but the three couples soon forged genuine friendships and often laughingly referred to themselves as "the Bottomleys," a respectful salute to the base of the cul-de-sac to which they owed their often chaotic but nonetheless contented lifestyle.

Carla made a conscious effort to listen rather than talk as she brewed coffee and placed some biscuits on a plate in front of Helena. "You know how much I love the house, Carlz, and the thought of leaving you too—it's awful. But there's no way around it. We'll have to use a good part of the money from the sale to fix up Mum's place and make a proper granny flat at the back. We want her to feel independent for as long as possible. The house will be ours eventually, of course, but living here has been … Well, who'd have thought, eh?"

"It's funny isn't it? The six of us are quite different. Perhaps that's why it works so well." Carla immediately felt another pang of guilt. Helena needed encouragement. "But let's face it, nothing can last forever. Not even when …" Oops, wrong again. This wasn't helping. Carla pulled out the chair next to Helena and sat down. "Helena, we're best friends. It's not the houses that matter really, is it? It's us. Nothing can stop us from remaining as close as we are now. Your mum's place is less than half an hour away. Lizzie and I can visit you, and the six of us can still get together." Helena returned Carla's smile and hastily wiped her eyes. Perhaps it needn't be so bad.

Carla hoped she sounded more confident than she felt. Helena always seemed the most vulnerable of the tight-knit group of friends. She had three children in as many years. The house was never quite tidy, and the garden was always a little unkempt. *People* mattered to Helena, and it showed. Carla slid the biscuit plate closer to her friend and took a bite from one herself in the hopes that the nauseating feeling in the pit of her stomach would settle. She would talk to Douglas tonight. He might be able to come up with a solution. Surely there had to be another option.

Douglas took his briefcase through to what once was the formal dining area but now operated as a study for both of them and placed it on the larger of the two desks in the room. "I saw the For Sale sign," he called out to Carla as he made his way toward the kitchen, where she was working. A pile of julienned vegetables was growing as she continued to chop green, red, and yellow capsicums. Smiling at Douglas as he came into the kitchen and planted a kiss firmly on her cheek, she raised her eyebrows in acknowledgement of his observation. "I suppose that's because of Helena's mum?"

"Yes," replied Carla, offering a slice of capsicum to Douglas and taking a bite of one herself.

"Well, I guess it had to happen sometime," he said as he took two glasses from the dresser and raised them to her in enquiry as to whether she intended to join him in a glass of wine. "All good things and all that," he added, regretting it instantly.

The doorbell sounded a quick double ring, signifying Lizzie's usual means of approach. Douglas put the glasses down and went to open the door, giving a good-humoured sidelong grin at Carla as he did so. Lizzie swept in, looking immaculate as always. An expensive silk shirt fell flatteringly over a pair of tight designer jeans. The heeled leather boots that completed the apparent artless look Lizzie favoured clicked across the nearly white entry tiles towards the kitchen. "They're moving!" she announced. "Helena, Greg, and the boys," she added unnecessarily. "They're moving!"

"Apparently." Carla rested the knife on the chopping board. "They need to move in with Helena's mum. She's close to needing full-time care now."

"But I thought her mum would come here." Lizzie wrapped her arms around herself as if she were cold.

"Perhaps they thought the upheaval for her mum would be a bit much. You know how Helena is."

"Yes, but … I wonder who we'll get," Lizzie said as Carla began chopping again.

"What do you mean?" asked Carla, rather confused.

"Well, I wonder who'll move in."

Carla stared at Lizzie open-mouthed and then turned towards Douglas. She had not considered the obvious for a single moment. If her best friend's family sold up and moved out, it followed that somebody else would move in. Another family would invade their idyllic existence. People they knew nothing about would expect to become part of their lives. She slowly sank down onto one of the bar stools that stood conveniently close to a collection of well-worn recipe books and burst into tears.

Douglas immediately crossed the room and wrapped his arms around her. "Don't cry, love. It'll be all right. Really. It'll be all right. I promise."

"Shit," said Lizzie. "Sorry."

CHAPTER 2

"I felt simply awful. Insensitive. Uncaring. Carla was distraught, and I was upset too. Just seeing the For Sale sign like that ..." Lizzie poured some water into a saucepan and put it on the stove to heat. Linguine with poached chicken was one of the default meals Lizzie sought consolation in when she was busy or stressed. "Of course, I ended up feeling like an absolute ... traitor ... almost."

"I'm sure you're overreacting. Carla knows how much you love her—and Helena." Mike poured them each a glass of wine and placed one on the workbench for Lizzie as she took butter from the fridge to make the sauce. "We're all close, but you three girls are practically joined at the hip. And it was a real shock driving up the street and seeing the sign. How did it go today, by the way, with the Porters? "Oh, good. They've decided to cut their losses and sell the business. It's definitely their best option." Mike and Lizzie both worked for the same law firm, but their areas of expertise differed. Lizzie drew up business contracts for new companies and dealt with business closures. Mike had gained a reputation for extreme attention to detail in the field of corporate law and sat on the boards of several big retail companies. Both careers had turned out to be lucrative. When they first married, they acknowledged that they were both considered "high-flyers," and they spent their money on extravagances without qualm.

Mike's father, Jim, also worked in law, and he had encouraged his son to follow a similar career path. To Mike's utter amazement, the father he held in such high regard came seriously undone in his late fifties. Jim was accused of insider trading and narrowly escaped a custodial prison sentence. He declared bankruptcy, lost his home, and was left without a job. Mary, Mike's mother, stuck by her husband throughout the entire ordeal, but she seemed to disappear behind a veil of shame. She became a mere shadow of her former self, without any trace of her previous vibrancy.

This whole event shocked Lizzie and Mike to the core and caused them to evaluate everything about their lifestyle. They both could see how easy it was to be carried away with financial success and to always require more to maintain a high income and the status that went with it. They agreed as one to take on an extra mortgage, allowing them to purchase a small house in a modest but pleasant suburb for Jim and Mary to live in. They had just moved into Capstan Court, and Lizzie had discovered she was pregnant. They loved the house and decided that they would make it their long-term home and be content with it. Their priorities would be each other and any other children they might have. Indulgences such as nice cars, designer clothes, and five star holidays were still affordable, but they shared a determination not to allow themselves to be drawn into a world that would risk such devastating loss.

They both heard a key turn in the lock. It was Sarah, home for the weekend. "Hi," she called as she made her way through to the kitchen. "Yum … I'm starving," she said, casting an appreciative eye over the half-prepared meal. Sarah had the same lithe body as her mother, but her hair was cropped short and she felt no need for makeup. She was naturally lovely but seemingly unaware of her power of attraction. Lizzie and Mike smiled as she moved towards her room, knowing that she planned to don a comfortable tracksuit in order to begin the process of chilling for the weekend break from study.

"Hey," Sarah called as she dumped her bag on her bed. "What's with the For Sale sign?" Lizzie and Mike looked at each other uncertainly.

"I wonder who'll move in," Sarah mused aloud.

"So … do you have plans or is this purely R and R?" enquired Lizzie. Sarah was making them a pot of tea later in the evening. Sarah was Lizzie and Mike's only child. Lizzie had been expecting a second when Sarah had just turned two. She was hoping for a boy, a pigeon pair. Seven months into the pregnancy, Lizzie became very ill. Rushed into hospital in agonising pain, she gave birth, but the baby only survived for a few hours. It was a boy. She and Mike were both broken-hearted. The doctors informed them the next day that it would be unlikely that they would be able to conceive again. Their friends from Capstan Court proved themselves true and genuine. They surrounded them with love and a generosity of heart that encompassed their grief and helped them continue. That incident had served to bind the six of them together so strongly.

"Both, really. Mostly chilling out, but I do have to go into town tomorrow."

"Shall we go together?" Lizzie proposed. She missed Sarah but was very conscious of the danger of appearing overbearing.

"No, sorry, Mum. That won't work. I'm meeting someone, I'm afraid."

"Oh. Anyone I know?" Lizzie enquired, avoiding eye contact as she poured from the pot.

"No. Just a friend. Do we have a biscuit to go with this tea? Preferably one that isn't good for us?"

Lizzie laughed and retrieved three custard tarts from the fridge. "Oh, I think we can do a little better than that. Don't you?"

CHAPTER 3

"The morning forecast was fine, so we should get at least one round in," said Greg as he loaded the three golfing bags into the back of his not too recent but nonetheless respectable and roomy hatchback.

Douglas seated himself comfortably in the back. "Sky looks okay to me. It's worth the risk." Mike nodded in agreement as he buckled up in the front passenger seat.

The three of them had a regular booking on the calendar for golf on Saturday mornings. They just took the one car, as they all enjoyed the typically male jocular tomfoolery that had become part of their relationship. They discussed everything from the current form of their favoured soccer teams to the vagaries of the stock market, from the antics of an errant politician to the state of the economy. They took turns on a tri-weekly basis to be the designated driver for the homeward journey, meaning they could linger over a few drinks at the bar without feeling guilty. Mike and Douglas always covered the cost of Greg's drinks, as his car was used regularly. This Saturday morning ritual had become entrenched in the psyche of the three couples and was rarely set aside for anything. Their wives had long since realised that the ritual in and of itself had little to do with the game of golf. The scores and handicaps were the mere vestiges of shared camaraderie.

Greg climbed into the driver's seat and buckled up. Cautiously backing out of the driveway as usual, he avoided making eye contact with either of the other two men. "Look, I'm really sorry about the upset. You know, you guys finding out about the sale once the sign was up …"

Douglas and Mike responded almost simultaneously with brief but genuine assurances of understanding.

"No, really. Helena has been putting off contacting anyone about the sale, and then it was me who said we shouldn't keep delaying things, so then she rang them. Before she knew it, there was this estate agent hammering the sign into the front garden. It wasn't meant to be like that at all …"

"Of course not, mate," Douglas said. "Carla just got a shock—that's all. She knows Helena has been under strain lately. Well, with her mum, I mean. It's no big deal."

"It's rotten for Helena. Well, for all the girls, isn't it?" added Mike. "They're so close you couldn't get a butter knife between them. But you aren't going to be far away. *Whoa*—check out the spoilers on that! It's a GTHO—"

"Yeah, Phase three," Douglas said. "Impressive or what?"

The sale of the Browne family home was, at least for the remainder of the morning, forgotten.

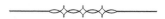

Carla considered Saturday mornings working hours. She had developed a small business that provided assistance around the home for people who might need it. Some patrons required help for a short time, perhaps following a spell in hospital or after the birth of a baby. Much of her clientele, however, consisted of regular customers prepared to pay for a variety of tasks to be undertaken by someone other than themselves. Carla prided herself on being prepared to supply a willing worker for almost any job. So long as it was legal and ethical, she'd find the right person to fit the bill. She knew lots of people who were happy to take on relatively small projects but who would rather not be responsible for a business themselves, and she knew a lot more who were happy to perform a variety of home duties for a little extra income.

Ben, Carla's son, earned enough money from his mother's business to see him through college so long as he remained living at home. He worked on anything to do with gardening, as he hoped to become a landscape gardener himself in about a year's time. Whenever brute force was required, perhaps dismantling or erecting a garden shed, for example, he would do that too. Ben's younger sister, Jeannie, did shopping, walked dogs, babysat children, and even bought and gift-wrapped presents occasionally, all in the name of saving for a trip that she intended to take with her best friend, Josie, when school was finally over.

"Good morning. Task Master. How may I help?" Carla was answering the second call of the morning. "Mrs. Young. Hello. What can I do for you?" Carla listened as Mrs. Young detailed what she needed done around the home in preparation for a ruby anniversary party. Taking all the details down carefully, Carla planted the thought in Mrs. Young's mind that she may find it useful to have a couple of people on hand at the party itself to assist with drinks, catering, clean-up, and so forth. Mrs. Young thought it was a brilliant idea, and Carla gave herself a mental pat on the back.

As pleased as she felt with herself over the potential earnings from Mrs. Young, Carla put the phone down with a heavy heart. She hadn't slept well for thinking about Helena's predicament. Douglas was right—nothing lasts forever, and she was best friends with a person, not a house, for heaven's sake. But somehow she knew that it wasn't that simple. Helena's moving away seemed like some sort of bad omen. The doorbell rang just as she had decided to make coffee before tackling the accounts for the week.

Helena stood on the doorstep holding a tin decorated with a Christmas snow scene that contained, Carla supposed, a fruit cake. "Have you got time for a coffee? I know you're usually busy on Saturday mornings, but I wondered if we could ask Lizzie in as well." Carla relieved Helena of the festive tin and suggested that she go next door to invite Lizzie over while she put the coffee on.

Within fifteen minutes, Helena and Lizzie had joined Carla and were sitting around her beloved self-renovated kitchen table with a coffee mug and a slice of fruit cake each. They had spent several of those fifteen minutes discussing a TV serial that had started the night before, comparing it to the book it was based on, which they had all read in their adolescent years. They were pulling apart the casting of the main characters. The conversation gradually ran out of steam. "I reckon you could sell this fruit cake, Helena," Carla ventured.

"The estate agent phoned first thing this morning," Helena said, tracing the line of a knot in the table with her finger. "He wants to hold a home open next weekend."

CHAPTER 4

The week prior to Sunday's home open, however, had not panned out as expected by any means. Carla had suggested to Ben and Jeannie that they offer a day's work each to Helena and Greg free of charge, allowing their mum to pay them for half a day. That way, they were expressing compassion in a practical way yet still gaining some reward for their hard work. Ben understood what needed to be done to get the garden up to scratch and make it look appealing to any prospective buyers. Jeannie would smarten up the inside of the house and hopefully make a few tasteful changes, exchanging its comfortable lived-in look for more of a trendy shabby chic feel. Helena's eldest son, Hugh, would supervise and work with his two younger brothers in tidying the garage. Carla assigned herself to the task of overseeing the whole project and keeping everyone on task and hydrated.

Helena took advantage of Lizzie's sense of style by having her accompany her to the HomeChic store on the edge of town in search of some bright cushions and a few other bits and pieces. The store seemed to run more or less continual specials, and besides, Helena could take them with her when they moved. Carla had managed to convince Douglas that the three guys should play golf as usual; otherwise, Helena would feel guilty about the whole effort, for both she and Greg needed a break.

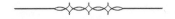

Helena counted herself very lucky to have her current job. She worked alongside Karen in the reception office at the school her boys attended. The two of them got on well together. Helena began her day at eight in the morning, took a half-hour lunch break, and finished at two in the afternoon. Her counterpart began at nine and finished at three. Although the beginning and end of the day were busy times in the office, Gina, the school principal, had introduced a policy whereby either herself or her assistant principal, Tania, were available in the office during those times. It worked successfully, as both of them were able to connect with any parents encountering concerns or issues, allowing them to cultivate an approachable demeanour with adults and students alike. Gina and Tania had in fact been partners for the last two years, but there was never any hint of their private relationship spilling over into their working lives. They both prided themselves on being strictly professional and managed the student body and its staff admirably.

Hugh was in his final year, and whilst he had not been particularly keen when faced with the prospect of moving out of Capstan Court, he understood that his grandmother probably shouldn't be living alone in a large house when she didn't enjoy particularly good health. As it happened, Grandma Betty lived a short distance from the school, and he couldn't see that it would make a huge difference concerning his last few months as a student. Louis and Davey were in years eleven and ten, respectively. Louis had sulked when he first received the news, but he adopted a more mature attitude in an attempt to appear as worldly-wise as his elder brother. Davey had made a huge song and dance about the whole thing. Everyone was rather sure it was mainly because he had a soft spot for Jeannie, even though she was his senior by a year.

On the Thursday morning before the home open, Helena answered the telephone and was surprised to hear a request to connect the caller to Mrs. Helena Browne.

"You are speaking to Helena Browne."

"Hello, Mrs. Browne. It's Parkway Hospital calling in regard to your mother, Mrs. Betty Dobson. According to our records, you're next of kin."

Helena's heart skipped a beat. "Yes. Is something wrong?"

"Mrs. Browne, your mother was admitted a short while ago as an emergency. I understand that she was talking to a neighbour when she suddenly appeared to turn very pale and became short of breath. Your mother's neighbour wasted no time in bringing her straight to the hospital, where she has been undergoing tests. The tests are not yet fully complete, but her neighbour is unable to stay here for much longer and has asked that we contact you."

"Yes. Yes, of course. I'll be there as soon as I can. Thank you." Helena sat there numb for several seconds, not being able to process fully what she needed to do. After taking a deep breath in order to regain her composure, she then walked calmly to the principal's office and knocked on the door.

Helena was working quite hard to maintain the facial expression and body language of a concerned but knowledgeable daughter. Once she saw Betty sitting up in bed with a cup of tea, she had relaxed immediately. In a short while, a female doctor who didn't look old enough to have finished school joined them. That same doctor was now explaining the current situation to Helena.

"Mrs. Browne." She smiled. "Thank you for coming in so promptly. Young Betty here gave her neighbour quite a shock!"

Helena was incensed at the patronising use of "young." Why not just use her name?

"We've done several tests and found nothing particularly untoward. Betty may have been simply standing for too long—without a hat," she added, smiling deliberately at Betty as if she should be issued with a warning notice. "Mrs. Dobson may be discharged, but I would prefer to know that someone will be there to keep an eye on her for, say, forty-eight hours."

"Of course. Naturally. No problem. I'll help Mum get dressed and we'll be on our way."

"Just be sure to call in at the desk before you leave to sign the discharge papers and so on."

"Yes. Thank you," Helena replied, somewhat irked, although she didn't really know why. She smiled warmly at her mother, who was just finishing her tea. "Home to my place, I think. We'll have a late lunch and then work out a plan of action." As she had expected, Gina hadn't hesitated in telling her to take the time she needed.

CHAPTER 5

Betty was lying on Helena's bed with the quilt that she had made several years ago as a gift for her daughter draped over her. She felt comfortable and cosy but was unable to "rest," as advised by Helena, for the thoughts running through her head. It was the cause of much personal chagrin for Betty that she was not enjoying full health in her latter years. The recent incident that had seen her distraught neighbour bundle Betty into her car and drive over the speed limit to the hospital, all the while assuring Betty that she was sure there was nothing to worry about and she shouldn't panic because they would shortly be in the best place possible if Betty needed urgent attention, had left her feeling embarrassed and foolish.

Sheila, Betty's neighbour, meant well, of course. Betty knew that. However, the rush to the hospital and the immediacy of the tests probably caused more anxiety for Betty than the initial feelings of lightheadedness and shortness of breath. Helena had to be called out of work. It all seemed so over the top. She felt like such a nuisance nowadays.

Rheumatoid arthritis caused Betty a lot of pain and discomfort. Lately she found difficulty in completing relatively simple household tasks. In addition, there had been a rather dramatic deterioration in her eyesight. Underlying the obvious physical evidence of ill health, she couldn't seem to fully shake off a sense of foreboding—about what, she didn't really know, but it dragged her down and made her feel miserable.

Born to a working-class family just after the war, Betty fulfilled her childhood dream of becoming a nurse once she left school. She knew on the first day on the ward that this was how she wanted to spend her life. Despite the bedpans and the unsavoury aspects of caring for those temporarily unable to care for themselves, she loved it. She found a real sense of purpose, but even more than that, she related to the patients for whom she cared with genuine empathy.

Bill's handsome face took precedence in her mind as she lay there trying to rest. That winning smile and the touch of sparkle behind the eyes had her hooked from the beginning. Bill had initially been admitted with appendicitis. The required operation had gone smoothly, but his wound became infected and his recovery took longer than expected. She knew that patients often fell in love with their nurses; she had experienced the phenomenon many times, as had most of her nursing friends. However "Once out the door, see them no more" was the norm. Betty became convinced, however, that this one was different. She was thoroughly swept off her feet, only to realise far too late that Bill really wanted a mother for his three rather unruly children. Susan, Timothy, and Thomas were being cared for by his mother following the untimely death of Bill's wife. They were to be reunited with him once he was on his feet again.

Bill was a builder—a good one. He bought bargain-priced houses, renovated them, and sold them for a good profit. The project he was currently working on held particular promise, as Bill intended to make it into a more than comfortable and spacious home for him and the children—and hopefully a new wife. In its original form, the modest brick and tile structure consisted of three bedrooms, a kitchen, bathroom, and a lounge room across the back. A laundry and sleep-out stood separately from the rest of the house. The block was a generous size, showing potential for an attractive garden and plenty of garage space.

Betty was thirty-eight when she accepted Bill's proposal. He was forty-five. They married six months later, when the house was fully renovated. The three children remained with Bill's mother until the house was ready, allowing Bill to concentrate on the project and speed up the completion date. It was shortly after they became a united household that Betty realised she had made a huge mistake. The children did not particularly take to her, and their father, when he was around, took their part in everything. They had been spoilt and had become used to living selfish existences, lacking respect for anyone else.

Much to Betty's delight, however, she discovered that she was pregnant at thirty-nine. Helena was the result, and she became the apple of Betty's eye. Bill had relatives in Canada, and one by one, his children went there to work, ending up emigrating. By the time Helena was eighteen, Betty, Bill, and Helena had the house to themselves. Life became more pleasant, and the three of them got on quite well. Bill no longer needed the money, but he kept working virtually every day God sent, except for one day each month, when he would partake in some kind of extreme sport. Skydiving, rock climbing, bungee jumping, and scuba diving gave him the thrill he seemed to need. It was on one rock-climbing jaunt that Bill died at the age of sixty-six. Ironically, it wasn't the rock climb that proved fatal. He collapsed in the bar of the clubroom and died in the ambulance of the way to the hospital.

Betty mourned her husband but always considered the real jewel in the crown to be Helena. In addition, she had a beautiful home and a very healthy bank balance.

"Would you like some sherry, Betty?" asked Greg as they settled down to chat after a dinner of roast chicken.

"Thank you, but no. Tea is wonderful." Betty loved Greg. He had always treated her kindly, right from the time he had started dating Helena. She had helped them both out with money a few times, although Greg had never asked. She was pleased to do it. When they first considered moving into Capstan Court, she had loaned them the deposit because she could see how much they loved the house. It took them a few years to pay it back, and they did so in dribs and drabs. Greg didn't command a particularly high salary as a hospital administrator, and sometimes it was tough making ends meet. Betty began a savings account for each of the three boys when they were born, which she hoped would set them up with a car each when the time was right. Her daughter's household wasn't a wealthy one, but it was happy.

"You, sweetie?" Greg asked Helena.

"No, thanks, love," she declined. Sinking into the chair, she rested her head back and closed her eyes. "I've given it some thought, Mum. If you stay here until Saturday, I'll take tomorrow off and then the plans for the home open can go ahead. After the boys have dealt with the shed, they'll pack a suitcase each. I'll take a quick trip to HomeChic with Lizzie, drop the stuff off for Jeannie, and take you back home. Greg can bring the boys over in the afternoon so they can settle in before school on Monday. Greg will stay here for the home open on Sunday."

"Have you spoken to the boys about it?" Greg was fixing himself a drink.

"Not yet, "said Helena, rubbing her temples and massaging her neck. "I'm picking my moment."

"Right." Greg took a liberal swallow of Scotch.

CHAPTER 6

"Think of it as a holiday!" cajoled Helena as she faced an annoyed Davey making his way to his room the next morning.

"Mum, I'm not ten, and I'm not stupid. I don't think I should have to go anywhere I don't want to go."

"Davey, please," she reasoned, reaching out to touch his arm before he squirmed away from her. "Why are you being uncooperative?"

"Because I don't want to go!" Davey shouted. He yanked open his bedroom door, walked inside, and slammed it shut.

Quite typically, Hugh had complied with his mother's request to pack a case once he had finished working on the garage. She always thought of him as the king of the philosophical approach. Louis took his lead from Hugh and gave his nodding assent. Davey was a different story.

Seeing no point in trying to reason with her youngest offspring, at least for the time being, Helena walked back into the kitchen, where Greg was washing up after breakfast. Carla had collected Betty so that she could spend the morning with her, allowing the clean-up tasks to get going. Helena and Lizzie went treasure hunting at HomeChic, and Greg, Douglas, and Mike set off for their usual game of golf.

Greg smiled encouragingly as Helena walked in. "That went well!"

"Not helpful, Greg," she replied. "I'd better get changed into something decent."

"Great day for a couple of rounds," Mike remarked as Greg turned left out of Capstan Court towards the main road. It was Mike's week as designated driver for the return trip.

Mike and Douglas exchanged comments about a current competition being held on their local radio station, called "Get Out!" Listeners called in with real-life experiences involving themselves and a celebrity. Every story that went to air won a scratch-and-win lotto ticket plus automatic entry into the most entertaining or remarkable encounter of the day as judged by the team of presenters, resulting in the prize of a double gold star cinema pass. Each of those winners then gained entry into the draw for a weekend in Melbourne, which included tickets to a stage show with a meet the cast drinks party thrown in.

"I've been trying to get Nina from the office to phone in," remarked Douglas. "Apparently, she was booked on a flight to Sydney, got upgraded to business class, and ended up sitting next to Paula Duncan, you know, from *What's It Worth*? Nina said she felt intimidated by her because she looked even more stunning in real life than she does on TV. In a rather misguided attempt to appear like a frequenter of business-class travel, she drank red wine virtually from the moment of take-off and got completely plastered.

"At some point, Ms Duncan gets up, presumably to answer the call of nature and fix her make-up before disembarking, and Nina manages to tip a full glass of red wine all over and then *into* this classy Gucci handbag that Paula Duncan is carrying. Speechless with shock and embarrassment, she just stares at Paula Duncan, who stares back at her. Slowly the wine seeps through the bag and drips onto Nina's lap as its unflappable owner, who still hasn't uttered a word, carries it across to the aisle. About ten minutes later, the aforementioned celebrity returns, accompanied by one of the flight attendants, who proceeds to settle her down into a vacant business-class seat on the other side of the aisle. A plastic bag, likely holding the wine-soaked designer bag, is tucked under the passenger seat in front of her. She gazes out the window.

"The attendant hands Nina an envelope and asks her if she can get her another glass of wine, which of course Nina refuses. When she finds the courage to open the envelope, she discovers a handwritten note: 'I sincerely apologise for my clumsiness. Please accept this small token as recompense for any damage caused to your clothing.' It was signed by Paula Duncan. Enclosed was a cheque for fifty dollars, which of course Nina never cashed."

"Far out!" Mike laughed.

"I think I've heard that story," said Greg.

"So which do you think?" asked Lizzie as she held two cushions side by side. "Orange and purple or the green and pink?"

"I love both, but I also really like that tall vase with the trailing lotus blossoms, so I think I'll opt for the green and pink. There's a table runner too." Helena was enjoying the shopping expedition to HomeChic. Lizzie had a real talent for home furnishings and decor, but she was making sure that the choices were all Helena's. Meanwhile, she was pointing out good bargains in an attempt to keep costs down. They had also spent a little on updating the kitchen workspace paraphernalia with a new spice rack, dish rack, and half a dozen bright tea towels.

They loaded up the boot of the car and set off for the return journey home. "I should have done this a while back. It seems a shame to only do this kind of thing when you're selling." She fell into a quiet reverie, and Lizzie tactfully changed the subject to the generous size of the parking bays in the car park.

Carla had enjoyed spending time with Betty. It had been a while since they had seen each other. Betty's movements definitely seemed to be more laboured, and when she was sitting with a selection of magazines to go through, Carla noticed that she was merely flicking through the pages and not attempting to read anything. When Carla decided to check on the progress next door, she found a movie for Betty to watch about the life of Monet and the legacy of his gardens that were made open to the public. Their TV screen was a large one, so Carla figured she should be able to view the movie adequately.

Walking from her home around to the front entrance of number 26, she was reminded of those few weeks almost twenty years ago when the three couples had moved in and started to get to know one another. She felt so genuinely thankful for the family lives they had shared, but when she reached the driveway, she felt overwhelmed with sadness that it was almost over. Not just for herself but for all of them, most of all for Helena. Her heart must be breaking. She wasn't just leaving a house; she was tearing asunder that unique bond that they knew.

Ben had done a marvellous job. The garden looked terrific. He had managed to create a tidy but not too manicured effect, creating the impression that the garden always looked as it did now. The pots of colour he had dug in close to the front door lent a bright and breezy atmosphere to the entrance.

"Well done, Ben. It looks fantastic!" Ben grinned at his mum and pretended to shine some imaginary medals fastened to his work shirt.

"Morning tea break in our kitchen in ten minutes," she advised.

Carla continued around to the garage at the back. Hugh, Louis, and Davey had decluttered the shed and tidied it, although she felt sure that Davey's efforts were not at all enthusiastic. She repeated her message regarding morning tea and agreed that they should accompany Ben to the tip with the full trailer following their partaking of refreshments. Entering the back door, she bumped into a cheery Jeannie, who promptly turned back into the house to show off her reorganisation designed to maximise the illusion of space. Carla was impressed. They walked back to the neighbouring property, where coffee had been brewing and was now ready for consumption.

Betty had dozed off, but she awoke as soon as everybody came into the kitchen. She made her way through to join them. A busy chatter accompanied the coffee and scones. However, Davey took his mug and plate outside and sat on the low garden wall, alone with his thoughts.

"Hey, Davey," Hugh said, interrupting Davey's solitude a few minutes later. "Ready for the dump off?"

"Reckon I'll give it a miss. You don't need me." Davey made his way towards the kitchen to return the crockery just as Jeannie was coming out.

"Hugh, did you come across anything in the garage that might be used for decoration?" asked Jeannie.

"Decoration?" repeated Hugh. "Like what?"

Davey suddenly brightened up. "I put a few things that I wasn't sure about chucking out on one of the shelves. Want me to show you?"

"Thanks." Jeannie glanced awkwardly at Hugh before following his younger brother. She had always liked Davey. They had gotten on well as children. He was sensitive, caring, and talented. She remembered when he got his classical guitar and seemed to take to it like a duck to water. She quite often heard him play, as the musical sounds would travel through his open bedroom window and reach out to her. Louis was nice enough, but he was quite often moody. Hugh—on the other hand—was, quite simply, gorgeous.

Davey showed her where he had put the rescued items. There weren't many: a couple of vases, a decorated basket, an old clock with an attractive wooden casing, and a white shallow cardboard box that was covered in dust and bore a Sweetnams label in the corner. "What's this?" Jeannie asked, taking the box down from the shelf and opening it.

"Oh," she said quietly, laying the lid on the shelf. "These are lovely!" She retrieved the table mats from their hiding place one by one. They each depicted an iconic Perth building. Hand-drawn and water-coloured, they had a pale pink background and a dark green border at their edges. A slightly lighter green script had been used to identify each structure. There were accompanying coasters to match.

Davey couldn't believe how delighted she was. "They're very old-fashioned, aren't they? I mean, people don't use stuff like that now, do they? I thought they might have been a wedding present or something and Mum might want to keep them."

Jeannie beamed at him. "That's the point, silly! I'm so glad you saved them. They would look fantastic mounted on the wall." She thanked him again and gave him a peck on the cheek. He felt his face blush and was mortified. "I can't wait to show them to your mum. I know just where they should go."

CHAPTER 7

"Do you mind if we drop these things off at my place straight away?" asked Helena as Lizzie pulled up on her driveway. She looked over at the garden. "Oh, Ben's been working really hard" Unloading the large bags from the car boot and awkwardly moving them into the house, they took them straight through into the sitting room. "Oh, yes, it looks more spacious with the sofas facing the windows. Jeannie has an eye ... obviously." Helena placed the bags she was carrying in the corner of the room and relieved Lizzie of her packages. "I'll set these out later, I think."

"Sure," said Lizzie. "Cup of tea next door, perhaps?"

"Well, I need the loo. You go. I must throw some things in a case ..."

After Lizzie had left, Helena looked out at the garden from the large window. It did look lovely, and the sofas positioned as they were took in the garden view. She removed the cushions from one of the bags and plumped them up before arranging them on the sofas. She admitted to herself that she preferred the room the way it was before.

Mike pulled up on the driveway a short time later. All three of them felt they should head straight home after just one round of drinks rather than dither at the bar.

"Wow," said Greg as he took in the garden. "Ben knows what he's doing."

"There might still be coffee next door," ventured Douglas, not wanting to make too much of the garden makeover.

"You two go, then. I'll check if Helena's here." As he made his way around the back of the house and into the kitchen, he also noted the neat and tidy garage. Greg had private nicknames for his three boys: Hewey, Dewey, and Lewey. He smiled to himself. They were good boys. He probably wouldn't be able to find anything in the garage now.

Helena was in the kitchen changing over some tea towels. She seemed to be replacing the familiar sights of Perth and other local landmarks worthy of tea towel notoriety with bright green and pink ones.

"Ooh, they look too good to use," commented Greg.

"Yes, I know. There's a table runner as well." Helena indicated it with a nod.

Greg noticed that all of the usual items kept on the table for everyday use were missing, presumably tidied away in cupboards. "Nice," he said.

Davey was resentfully throwing some things into a large holdall that was normally reserved for school camps. He truly was fed up with being told what to do. Davey loved Grandma Betty and was sorry she was ill, but it wasn't his fault. He looked around his room. It was organised in a messy kind of a way. He knew where everything was, and he never failed to put his dirty clothes in the laundry basket. Just recently, Helena had wanted the boys to update their doona covers. They were free to select their own designs. Hugh opted for plain black, Louis chose grey with a white stripe, and Davey refused to change his. It had a grey background, sets of five black lines forming musical staves, large black musical notes dotted along each stave and several guitar images obscuring everything behind them. It had been a birthday gift two years ago, and he wanted it to stay.

The corner of his room that was the least messy held his guitar on a stand and a wooden blanket box filled with sheet music, guitar lesson manuals, strings, plectrums, and, as he often quoted to himself, "much more!" He favoured classical guitar, and when he was absorbed in the music he was playing, he felt right with the world. Sometimes he composed his own tunes. The latest piece he had worked on consisted of simple, light melodic phrases that danced over a single repetitive note. It reminded him of Jeannie.

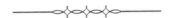

"Take your time, Mum. Make sure each move is complete before taking another." Helena was assisting her mother into her small runabout. She had packed a case but only worried about clothing and essentials for the moment. Greg would follow later with the boys and then return home. He wanted to be available to talk to the real estate agent in person after the home open the following day. Betty's hospital incident had thrown everything off kilter, but it couldn't be helped. Her mum dozed off about halfway through the journey, leaving Helena alone with her muddled and rather half-baked thoughts.

It was almost dinner time when Greg arrived with the boys, so Helena opened several cans of soup (she wondered if Betty had been virtually living on tinned soup). She sent the boys to the deli close by to pick up some crusty bread and cheese, and they shared a makeshift meal around the kitchen table. Once they had eaten, Helena sent them off with instructions to work out for themselves who was sleeping where. There were plenty of beds, and for the time being, they were making do with sleeping bags and pillows from home. One spare bed in a small room adjacent to Betty's was always made up in anticipation of an unexpected guest, and Helena had reserved that one for herself by placing her case on it. Surprisingly, Hugh and Louis did seem to be treating it as a holiday. Davey had hardly spoken a word.

Greg noted that the boys were busily engaged. "I'll go home now and ring you tomorrow after I've spoken to the agent. OK?"

"Do you really need to go now?" asked Helena.

"Yeah, I probably should just check the house over, you know. I'm not sure how the boys left their rooms …" Greg began clearing the table. "I'll help you with this lot first, though." Whilst they worked together, Greg related Douglas's story about the on-flight celebrity encounter, and for a short while, they were on the same page, laughing together.

Betty got up to fill the kettle. It was funny how she could achieve some tasks without hesitation.

"So you've chosen the apartment!" Helena commented, referring to the annex that served as a laundry and enclosed sleep-out.

"I've not chosen anything," Davey mumbled. "This really is friggin' unfair, Mum."

Helena was trying to think of the wisest thing to say when Hugh burst into the room. "Hey, Mum. There's a rock expo at the stadium tomorrow. We'll all go and get out of your hair for the day."

"Terrific," said Helena, smiling wanly.

Helena usually loved Sundays. She and Greg would often linger in bed and have a "compare the week" discussion that usually turned into a lighthearted competition of the best and worst aspects of their week. They would cook breakfast together and work on the quiz in the newspaper. The boys were often out with friends or sometimes they would bring friends over. One shelf in the pantry was a freebie shelf. Anything from there could be consumed without asking permission, and there was a strict clear-up-after-yourselves rule on Sundays. In the afternoon, they might go for a walk or a ride. Around six o'clock, enough jacket potatoes for whoever was at home were put into the oven and served later with butter and cheese. This comforting routine had gradually developed over the years as their family had grown. It had helped them all stay sane amongst the busyness of their lives.

This Sunday was different. Helena was missing Greg and feeling anxious about the home open. She was worried about Davey, even though he had left the house in quite a buoyant mood with Hugh and Louis. Betty seemed to be behaving oddly. Normally she was full of chat, but she spent most of the day in either her bedroom or slowly walking around the garden. Currently she was watching a repeat episode of *Glorious Gardens* on TV.

Greg didn't phone until late afternoon. Apparently, there had been quite a few people viewing the house, but the agent felt only one couple were seriously interested in purchasing. However, three clients wished to view it during the week. Greg insisted on staying at the house until next weekend.

The boys returned at six thirty expecting jacket potatoes to be on the go, but Helena had completely forgotten about preparing a meal. They phoned for pizza.

CHAPTER 8

Helena awoke with a start. A panicked glance at the clock on the bedside table informed her that she was late—but not horribly late. She could hear the familiar sounds of breakfast preparation going on in the kitchen and so presumed the boys were doing the right thing and getting ready for school, probably being stirred by Hugh.

Grabbing her dressing gown, Helena went out to the kitchen to assure them all she would be ready to go in ten minutes. Betty was making tea, and the three boys were eating generous helpings of cereal.

"Davey, why aren't you in uniform?"

"I forgot to pack it," he said with a mouthful of cereal.

"What do you mean, you forgot to pack it?" Helena felt her voice rising.

"I mean, I forgot to pack it," said Davey matter-of-factly.

"Oh, Davey." Helena briskly ran her fingers through her hair. Hugh and Louis both took their bowls to the sink and washed them.

"Don't worry. I'll ask Dad to drop it off sometime tonight; then I'll have it for the morning. I can miss school today."

This was such a calculated move. Helena was speechless. Davey knew how strict the school was about uniform.

"You'd better hurry or you'll be late," Davey said, "and so will everyone else." He picked up his bowl, carried it to the sink, washed it, returned to his room, and closed the door.

Everyone else seemed to be operating under a code of silence. She looked at them one by one, but they were studiously avoiding her gaze.

Betty was feeling virtually invisible. The boys had always treated her well, and she knew they loved her. But at the moment, apart from the occasional "Hello, Gran" or "Thanks, Gran," she was practically ignored. Even Helena seemed taken up with her own thoughts, and the easy conversation they usually enjoyed was conspicuous in its absence. She made her tea and took it through to her bedroom, which had space enough for a comfortable recliner. Apart from her prescription medication, which she had to admit gave her several hours of semi-relief, this certainly assisted with the ongoing pain she had to cope with. She found that the best antidote was to become absorbed in something else. She read large-print books from the local library, which her neighbour Irene picked up and returned for her. Sometimes Irene would include an audiobook. She listened to the radio, particularly Channel Triple 3, which played music she remembered from her younger days. She did a quiz every afternoon and often interviewed interesting guests.

Resting her cup carefully on the coffee table next to her recliner, she took a few moments to settle herself into her chair and then picked up the phone. She had a couple of calls to make.

Helena was livid. Hugh and Louis were seated in the rear of the car and comparing notes about a student teacher they had experienced the week before, chatting as if nothing untoward had happened. They must have been in on the plan. Well, she wasn't going to dignify their malcontent by showing her anger; they could … She hit the brakes suddenly and screeched to a halt. She had almost run a red light. The driver of the car behind her blasted her with his horn.

"Woah … take it easy, Mum!" said Louis. She felt like telling them to get out of the car and walk the rest of the bloody way on foot. Instead, she aimed a swear word that was strictly banned in their household directly at the windscreen. Hugh and Louis looked at each other, pulled amused faces, and stifled their laughter.

They arrived in the school car park just as the morning siren sounded. The boys weren't late, but Helena was. Feeling bad about the earlier incident, Helena apologised and they shared a quick hug.

"Dammit. You've no lunches!" A twenty-dollar note was quickly retrieved from their mother's purse and passed on to Hugh.

"Bonus," said Louis.

Making her way across the car park toward the office, Helena made a concerted effort to calm down and prepare herself for the working day. One of the principal's mantras was "Stressed staff create stressed parents." Entering through the main door, she crossed the reception area and knocked on Gina's door. Rather than call out to people, Gina preferred to open the door and greet her caller with a warm smile and say pleasantly, "Please come in."

"Ah, Helena! How are things? How is your mother?"

"Mother is not too bad at all, really. Both of her neighbours are calling in to her mid-morning and mid-afternoon, and I shall phone at lunchtime to check. To be honest we are all struggling more than she is, I think."

"Ageing parents can definitely be a problem. But I encourage you not to do anything hasty. It's nothing to do with me, I know, but you are a valued staff member, Helena. I'm always here to talk if you need to. Remember that."

Helena thanked her and left the office. She loved this job. A silent prayer was sent heavenward as she took her regular place behind the reception desk.

"Sorry to keep you waiting, Mrs. Bell. Do you have that permission slip for Dana?"

Greg was listening patiently to Mr. Wilson as he related the sorry tale of his guide dog's unexpected demise, coupled with the annoyance he was experiencing with his sister, who was, in his view, a complete hypochondriac. Neither tale had anything whatsoever to do with the payment of an outstanding medical bill, which was the reason for his presence opposite Greg at the chief administrator's desk of the Brothers of Mercy Hospital. He was dealing with it himself rather than leaving it up to one of the regular clerks because there had been a problem with the previous bill and Mr. Wilson had complained. Greg found that most people appreciated the sense of gravitas that accompanied the introduction of his name and title, along with a polite handshake when an error needed to be rectified. Normally he was prepared to listen, as that was an essential part of effective customer relations, but today he was not sorry to bid farewell to a hopefully appeased client.

The phone rang, and Greg excused himself from Mr. Wilson, who stood to leave.

"Mr. Browne, there's a call from your son Davey on line three."

"Thank you, Mrs. Young. I shall start on the preparations tomorrow and keep you informed as to what is going on. I am confident that it will be a wonderful celebration, and you know, you are so wise to delegate as much of the organisation as you can. Otherwise, the worry just spoils your own enjoyment of the day."

Carla hung up after they had both issued goodbyes. She was pleased with the prospect of this coming event, even though it was short notice. It was particularly satisfying to be managing a whole project rather than odd bits and pieces, although Carla was well aware that the small regular jobs had served to build up a client base as well as a reliable group of part-time workers without too much stress. Mrs. Young was prepared to spend money, and Carla knew that if this party was successful, it could lead to several recommendations. It did have to be done well, however. This client had high expectations.

"Davey, I sympathise, but I have to say I'm not happy with you deliberately causing your mother all that unnecessary hassle." A few moments of silence hung between Davey and his Dad.

"Look, I'll leave work at about three and I'll come and pick you up. Be ready. You can stay home with me for now, *but* your room has to be kept tidy. In fact, everything has to be kept tidy. You'll have to catch the bus, which will add a good twenty minutes each way to your school day."

"Cool. Thanks, Dad. I owe you one."

"No, actually, you owe your mother a sincere apology."

CHAPTER 9

Louis and Hugh had to admit that Davey had pulled a neat stunt. No shouting match, not even a raised voice. A statement of fact and the presentation of a fait accompli. Brilliant. The two older boys had not been involved at all. They were surprised to see him eating breakfast dressed in jeans and a T-shirt, but they made no comment. What had been unexpected was their dad agreeing to take him back home and acceding to his staying, with a few minor provisos. The two of them concurred that they would give it until the weekend and then approach Greg about returning home themselves.

Hugh wasn't particularly keen on staying at Grandma Betty's. There were friends who lived nearby, but somehow it wasn't the same. He couldn't invite people back to Betty's place, and there was stuff in his own room that he liked having around him.

Louis quite liked the idea of travelling by bus to and from school. Many of his mates travelled by bus.

"Next door looks really great," said Lizzie to Carla. "Ben did a great job and so did Jeannie. Those table mats and coasters look fantastic." Ben knew how to mount them, and they had been given pride of place in the entry to very good effect. The six large placemats complemented an entire wall, and Ben had placed a lush looking green fern beneath them. The opposite wall housed a large mirror. The coasters mounted on one side of it echoed the large mats perfectly. The result was stylish rather than showy.

"It's odd, though, isn't it? Helena not being here. It's horrible that she's felt she had to move out before they even *had* to move out."

"It's very odd. I can't even work it out," Carla commented. "I did notice that Betty was slower when she was here with me, and her eyes aren't too good—but full-time care? I'm not convinced that she needs that just yet. There's all this upheaval going on, and I'm not sure it's really been thought through. Hey, you know Mrs. Young from Castle Gardens? She's holding a ruby wedding. Guess who's got the planning contract?"

"Oh, I can't possibly guess," teased Lizzie. "Would it be you, by any chance?"

"I've not taken Davey's side against you, love. He was really unhappy. There's been a consequence. He has to catch the bus, which to be honest will probably do him good anyway. We've all got carried away too quickly with this whole thing …"

"But I've no choice, Greg," Helena blurted out. "Betty is my mother, and she is going to get worse rather than better. She's helped us out lots of times, and now we need to help her."

Greg sighed heavily on his end of the line.

"It's like you've left me, Greg," Helena said quietly.

"No, actually. You've left me."

Betty had remained in contact with two close friends from her nursing days. Marinda was younger by several years. They had met working at the same hospital, but Marinda had gone on to run an indigenous health centre with great efficiency and compassion. She earned the respect of her aboriginal clients and their families as well as the admiration of the doctors and social workers she managed to persuade to donating time to the centre on a regular basis. Somehow, she had managed to raise four children as well. Joan was a year younger than Betty and enjoyed good health. She maintained that her well-being was due to never having married. Both Marinda and Joan now resided in Northam.

Having spoken to Marinda on the phone for quite some time, Betty felt reassured. Despite being conscious that she had a good deal of common sense herself, Betty found her emotions and gut feelings tangled up with practicalities; she needed an understanding soul to confide in. When Sheila from next door dropped in to check on her, she would ask if they could possibly take a trip to the closest pharmacist.

Tuesday turned out to be a day of surprises for Davey. Walking to the bus stop, catching the bus, and chatting with his mates on both journeys felt good. Autonomous, he decided. Late in the afternoon, his guitar practise was interrupted by someone knocking on the front door. He was pleased to see Jeannie standing there, and he was also pleased to note that he had not sensed that awful rush of awkwardness resulting in blushing like blazes.

"Hi, Jeannie. Come in." He gestured towards the newly mounted placemats and coasters on the wall. "Have you come to admire the decor?" he asked, quite impressed with how together he was sounding.

"They do look great, don't they? Good one, Davey. But Mum sent me around here to ask you something. She thought it would be better coming from me."

"Oh, right." Probably someone needed dustbins emptied on a regular basis or a pet hamster fed.

"Mum's got this job coming up. She's excited, you know—all fired up, wants it to go without a hitch and all. Well, she needs mood music for a ruby anniversary party, and she thought of you. Well, you and your guitar, that is." Jeannie smiled winningly.

"Seriously? She wants me to play my guitar … for money?"

"Yes. She said you have to understand that it's not a concert. People won't be there to listen to you. You will be providing 'ambience.'" She giggled. "What do you think?"

"What do I think?" He grinned expansively. "Today a ruby wedding party. Tomorrow …?" He tapered off a little awkwardly, as he couldn't think of a suitable punchline. This was so cool.

"Great. I'll tell Mum, then. She'll be so pleased. I'm waitressing, of course. It's boring, but it pays. Well, I must get back. Thanks."

Davey closed the door feeling as if he'd just won *The Entire Western Hemisphere Has Got Talent*. He punched the air several times before returning to his room to search out some suitable music. His first gig. He hadn't even asked when and where. "Tomorrow—Carnegie Hall" was what he should have said, he realised belatedly.

Helena unloaded the shopping bags from the car and took them through to Betty's kitchen, ready to begin the tedious task of putting everything away. She called out to her mother as she set the first few bags on the counter. The boys followed with the rest, dumped them rather unceremoniously, and, removing a bag of corn chips from the freshly purchased groceries, took it outside. She was about to remark that they could help with the packing away when Betty came out of her room. Helena was a little taken aback, as she appeared to have added a slick of lipstick and was proudly supporting herself with a stick—and were those new shoes?

"Hello, darling. I can help you with that," she said as she approached the workbench and rested her stick against the handle of the top drawer. "How about I sort and you stack?"

"Thanks," said Helena, wondering quite how to respond.

"What do you think of my new fashion accessories? I feel considerably firmer afoot in these shoes. The girl at the pharmacy was so helpful. There's quite a good range of styles nowadays. I'm still practising with the walking aid, of course. Finding the best place to rest it takes a bit of thought."

"You're a dark horse!" Helena remarked, recovering herself. "New lipstick too?"

"Well, while I was there …" Betty shrugged a little sheepishly.

"Who took you to the pharmacy?"

"Sheila from next door. She bought some shoes as well!"

Davey casually intended to mention the news about his first prospective gig to his dad over dinner. But as soon as Greg walked in, he was greeted by an effervescent son bearing an extremely wide grin. Davey related the news, and his dad responded with an appropriate level of excitement and enthusiasm.

"I guess we need to be out of the house while the agent is here," Greg said, moving through to the desk located in an alcove in the corner of the lounge room. "How about I treat us to Chinese?"

"Bonus," said Davey, still beaming.

"Don't get used to it. Most musicians are either half-starved and living off handouts from their grandmothers or stacking shelves on a midnight shift," he cautioned good-naturedly. "I'll just check my emails and get changed."

Helena and Betty were watching a TV documentary about homeless dogs. Helena's mind was all over the place. The boys had (she supposed) completed any homework and were playing ping-pong at a table that had been secreted behind the bed in the annex. She knew it wouldn't be long before they went back home.

She didn't know quite how she had gotten herself into this mess. Now she couldn't see how she could abandon her mother, even with the new shoes and the walking stick, she mused wryly. Both neighbours were willing to keep an eye on Betty during the day, but would she be capable of making decent meals, cleaning the house, changing bedding, and doing all those chores necessary when living alone? It was doubtful.

Of course, as Carla always said, you can pay someone to do almost anything, but she and Greg couldn't afford to pay people to cover so many tasks. And whilst she was sure her mother was not short of money, was it fair to expect her to do that when the house was roomy enough for them all to move in, even without a granny flat?

CHAPTER 10

"You do realise that the guests at this party aren't there for you, don't you, Davey? You must be smartly dressed and unobtrusive. Carla is taking on a risk—you mustn't let her down."

"Yeah, I know. I'll take it all seriously, Dad, honestly." He scooped up a forkful of sweet-and-sour chicken and grinned at his Dad again.

Greg was intrigued. It was as if he was seeing a completely new Davey. He appeared to be walking taller and speaking more confidently. He hadn't stopped grinning all evening.

He and Helena knew that Hugh was clever. He sailed through his schoolwork and managed to stay on the right side of the teaching staff. He had been tutoring for the last few years to earn some money and was anticipating entry into university to study pharmacy.

Louis was bright too, but he lacked the people skills of his elder brother and sometimes rubbed people up the wrong way, but he was learning to think before he spoke, although he wasn't speaking overly much at present. Rather, he seemed to consider a shrug and a grunt as sufficient means of communication. He had a tendency to sulk, which drove both Helena and Greg mad.

Davey was quieter than the other two boys. Whilst both parents were aware that he had musical talent, they did not make too much of it because they wanted him to have a stable career to fall back on. But they had to admit that it seemed to be music that brought him to life. It was part of his very soul.

"Have you told your mum yet?"

"No, not yet."

"And have you apologised?"

"N-nnoo."

"Do both now, please," said Greg, handing him the phone.

Carla had determined from the very beginning that everything to do with her small business would be undertaken with a professional attitude. No one was given a task to do without the accompanying paperwork that listed details, requirements, and expected remuneration. It was the same for the clients. She upheld the same rules for her own children when they worked for her, and she expected them to behave responsibly.

Mrs. Young and her two daughters wanted to do the catering for the party themselves. It was all sweet and savoury finger foods, and following the latest trend, the celebratory cake was to be comprised of forty cupcakes complete with cream-coloured icing and deep red decorative baubles. Carla decided on two waiting staff. Jeannie and Josie would initially be handing out drinks on trays to guests as they arrived and then move on to platters of finger foods as the party got underway. Pleased that Davey had taken up the offer of providing mood music, she was able to picture in her mind a rather sophisticated affair that was almost bound to result in recommendations.

One section of the staff booking forms designed by Carla was devoted to "suitable attire." More often than not, the notation would read *comfortable clothing*. This time Carla was filling in *smart black* for Jeannie, Josie, and Davey.

Guests were due to arrive at seven that evening. Carla insisted that her three assistants meet at Carla's house at six so she could check their appearance. She did not feel anxious about the two girls but wanted to ensure that Davey was dressed appropriately and was fully prepared from a musical standpoint. (She needed to locate some back-up music to allow Davey a break when necessary.) The four of them would arrive together at least twenty minutes before seven, thus reassuring Mrs. Young that the evening would flow smoothly.

An appointment at Mrs. Young's home had been arranged to discuss the house decorations along with how best to create an atmosphere promoting that buzz of easy interactive conversation indicative of a successful event. In a way, Carla was glad of the short notice. There was less time to be nervous and over plan. She was keen and excited, but she counselled herself to be calm in Mrs. Young's presence, consolidating the impression that she was fully in control.

"Mary?" said Mike, somewhat surprised. It was unusual for his mother to phone, and he couldn't recall another time when she had phoned him at work.

"Yes, sorry. I know you're working. I won't keep you. I just … wondered if you could call in tonight for a while …"

"Is something wrong, Mary?"

"No, no. I just wanted to … run something by you … if that's OK."

"Of course." Mike felt distinctly uneasy, but obviously Mary didn't want to talk on the phone, and he was due in a meeting anyway. "How about eight o'clock, then?"

"Lovely. I'll see you at eight."

"I'd love to waitress with you, Jeannie. Tell your mum, yes, please!" Josie and Jeannie had been good friends for years. "I bet your mum's rapt. Party planning!"

"Ew," they chorused together, pouting and shaking their hips in an exaggerated fashion, in perfect sync with one another.

"What must we wear?" asked Josie.

"Smart black," quoted Jeannie. "And modest, of course."

"Of course," Josie reiterated. "Positively virginal."

"Ew," they both repeated, laughing conspiratorially.

"What's up with you two?" It was Cecily. Having recently relocated, she was quite new to the school and was keen to get in with Jeannie and Josie, as they were annoyingly popular with the girls and, more importantly, the boys.

Josie explained briefly about their upcoming job.

"Oh, yeah. I've done a bit of that. Easy money, really. Tell your mum I'll do it whenever she wants."

Cecily spied Robert walking back from the canteen. "Hey, Robert. What's up with you? Got something to share?" Robert grinned foolishly and offered her some potato chips from the bag he had just opened. She took several.

"I'll be sure to tell Mum—*not*," Jeannie mouthed to Josie just as the siren sounded.

"So what happened with Mary? Is everything all right?" Lizzie asked Mike as they were getting into bed later that night.

Mike and Lizzie had dispensed with the Mum and Dad monikers for Jim and Mary whilst the trauma of the bankruptcy had been going on. It was a calculated move, in a way. Mike seemed to feel that he needed to interact with Jim on an equal footing, almost businesslike, if this complicated situation was to be resolved satisfactorily. Lizzie had taken her lead from Mike.

"Not really, no." Mike had just stepped out of the shower. Lizzie loved the way he looked after a shower. His hair was unkempt rather than untidy. That and the stubble that became evident at this time of the day enhanced the rugged good looks of a man who obviously took good care of himself. He jogged a couple of times a week and was quite disciplined with regard to what he ate and drank.

Lizzie became concerned. "Tell me."

"Well, this is the thing. I'm not sure what I can tell you. Mary wasn't sure what she was telling me either. She says that Jim is being evasive. Secretive, was how she put it. He's going out without saying exactly where he's going and returning looking rather flushed and excited, apparently. And he is being cautious about money, not wanting to spend it on the things they usually would, like a Chinese meal or a movie. She didn't say as much, but I think she's worried that he might be straying or—and I don't know which is worse—gambling."

"Oh my God, Mike. That's awful. Poor Mary. What will you do?"

"I haven't got the faintest idea," Mike said as he climbed into bed beside Lizzie and propped himself up on his side, looking at her intently. "But I do know what I'm going to do right now," he said as he slipped the thin strap of her silk nightdress off her shoulder. "You are so beautiful. You know that, don't you?"

"You might have to tell me a few more times," she said, moving closer. "I need to be thoroughly convinced."

CHAPTER 11

Carla was in town making one of her visits to Flamboyant. The store was run by a woman named Dolores (Carla was pretty sure her given name was in actual fact Dorothy, having caught sight of a printed delivery invoice on the counter one day when she was waiting to pay). The sonorous Dolores exuded an expansive style of customer service that matched the store's name. The business was stocked with labels that were a cut above the average yet affordable, and she had built up a solid clientele base.

Her attractive window presentations often caught the eye of the casual shopper on a day out. At the rear of the premises, a rack of clothing items encompassed its entire length apart from a generously proportioned changing room at each end. This rack featured an eclectic mix of garments described by the proprietor as vintage. Most of them were simply second-hand goods or fashions from the previous year. Dolores had contacts, and she knew what would sell and what wouldn't. Carla simply loved the place. A discerning eye resulted in an unusual yet elegant wardrobe that was not overstuffed with hardly-ever-worn pieces of clothing. A couple of smart jackets served to lend a professional touch, and her purchases remained within budget.

"Hello, my dear. It's good to see you again," Dolores purred. "I have a few recently arrived specials that I'm sure will appeal to you." She then led the way towards the back of the store. "My regular customers can take an extra ten percent off," she added with an indulgent smile aimed at Carla but intended to reach the other two women in the store. Retrieving an almost ankle-length faux suede black skirt from the rack and hanging it on the rail of one of the changing rooms, she deftly pulled out two tops and hung one each on either side of the skirt. Both were silk and three-quarter sleeved but with completely different looks. The first was a burnt orange shirt with concealed buttons and a subtle leaf design in soft grey. The second was a deep charcoal fitted top, edged in white, with a laced panel over each shoulder in the same shade of charcoal. They were both stunning.

"Where do you find these things?" enquired Carla, knowing she would not get an answer.

"Shall I leave you to try them on? Do let me see—I like to know my instincts are well honed," she laughed, taking in the other customers once more. Regular patrons like Carla were worth their weight in gold.

Carla left the store with all three items encased in an environmentally friendly reusable bag and made her way towards the crossing. About fifty metres farther down on the opposite side of the street, there was a pleasant little cafe. Glancing at her watch, she decided there was definitely time for a cup of tea, maybe even two. Suddenly, she became aware of a familiar figure several metres ahead of her. Was that Sarah?

A short and rather dumpy woman struggling to restrain three excitable dogs on separate leads came towards her and watched on helplessly as two dogs went on one side of Carla whilst the third swayed away uncertainly apart from the others and took a tour around Carla in the other direction. It took a while for both Carla and the dogs' owner to extricate themselves, the mutts, and the leads from the resultant tangle, enabling Carla to continue on her way.

Looking ahead, she saw the familiar sights of the bank with its line-up of usual suspects waiting for a turn at the ATM, a cut-price store drawing attention to itself by way of sticky backed gold stars adhered to the windows, Sunvast Travel boasting enticing specials to faraway places, and the gourmet butchers, but no Sarah. She was probably mistaken anyway. It would be unusual for Sarah to be in town on a weekday, she would imagine.

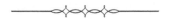

Greg was giving himself a metaphorical kicking. Why the blazes had he suggested that they needed to get a move on with regard to Betty's situation rather than let sleeping dogs lie? Before he knew it, that damned sign had been hammered in. It felt as if their lives had been shattered along with it.

Greg had never known his father. His mother raised him alone and did the absolute best that she knew how to do, but was never able to own a home. Rather, they had frequently moved house during his formative years, as was often the way with rental accommodation. He vowed that his own family would know the stability and consistency of a much-loved home and not feel under any pressure to move out before the time felt right for them. When he and Helena had found the house in Capstan Court, they fell in love with it. Betty's generous loan, for which Greg would forever be grateful, secured their purchase and they moved in. It had been a dream come true, but now the dream was turning into a nightmare.

"The agent said the young couple seemed 'quite keen although they had other properties to view and would I consider dropping the price?' Bollocks to that."

There was a real edge to Greg's voice, Helena noted, as they spoke on the phone that evening. "There are two more to go this week, aren't there?" She had taken the phone into the annex and was idly brushing dust off the edge of the ping-pong table. "Are you coming here for dinner tomorrow night?"

"No, Davey and I are having a go at a Thai green curry."

"Oh."

"At the *pub*?" Jim repeated, arching his eyebrows and looking enquiringly at Mary, who suddenly appeared to notice a greasy mark on the fridge door. She crossed to the kitchen sink and picking up a cloth and spray bottle hastily set about polishing the daylights out of the shiny surface of the offensive appliance. "Which pub?" he continued. "We don't normally go to the pub. I didn't think you liked pubs. Why can't you come here for a coffee? Or a beer, if you really want to. You could bring us both a beer."

"Well, sometimes it's good to get out of the house, isn't it? I thought The Feathers or The Maiden. Which would you prefer?" prompted Mike.

"I don't know, do I? I don't go to the pub. Are you feeling all right, son?"

"Of course I'm all right." This wasn't going well. "Surely I can take my father to the pub without getting the third degree? I think The Maiden does good counter meals."

"Counter meals?" Jim responded. "Oh, I don't want a counter meal. Why would I want a counter meal?"

"Mary might appreciate a night off cooking, don't you think?"

"Well, Mary isn't coming, is she? So she'd have to cook for herself anyway, wouldn't she?"

Mike was about to give up in frustration. Why was this so hard? He'd thought his father would jump at the chance. "A restaurant, then?"

"Oh, no. Not a restaurant. If you really want to go to the pub, I'll go. You choose which one. Will you pick me up?"

Mike arranged the details with his father, grateful for his eventual compliance. He'd chosen The Feathers, and he'd pick him up at a quarter after seven the following night. There would be no meal. They could talk man to man, Mike hoped, although if the previous conversation was anything to go by, he might be on a losing wicket.

Jim hit the OFF button on his phone and looked at Mary, who had moved on from the marked refrigerator and was adding teabags to the caddy. "I'm a bit worried about Mike," he said. "I didn't think he liked pubs."

CHAPTER 12

Helena attempted a note of enthusiasm with Hugh and Louis at breakfast time. "What would you think about a curry night?" she suggested brightly.

"Um, well, hockey training starts again tonight, remember?" She hadn't remembered. She was having a tough time remembering which day of the week it was. Hugh noticed the disappointment in his mum's face. "We'll be late, about seven, but we could do a curry night if you really want to."

"We usually have pies on training nights, don't we? I like pies …" Louis felt his brothers' gaze rest on him, and he looked across to see Hugh nod almost imperceptibly in his mother's direction. "Curry is OK, though. We can have curry … if you want curry."

"No." Helena looked apologetically at them both. "I'm sorry. I wasn't thinking. Pies it will be."

"Curry another night, then?" suggested Hugh with a pang of guilt, knowing full well that they both planned to have returned home by the weekend.

"I agree," said Carla to Mrs. Young on the phone later that day. "People prefer to have a designated zone for jackets and so on. That room at the front of the house leads into a small en suite, which allows privacy. You could even put a discrete restroom sign on the ensuite door. If we set up our musician close by the cloakroom, it also suggests a certain amount of security, as he can observed people coming and going by him. I also think a small table on which people may place any gifts as they enter is a good idea. Wrap up a small empty box or two and place them on the table to signify its use. Also, I shall bring a complimentary guest book along for people to sign, which I suggest sits on the same table. It makes a nice memento for yourselves and sends a message to your guests that you value their presence." Carla had spied a rather nice guest book in the cut-price shop in town and had purchased it and a couple of gold gel pens in anticipation.

"As people move through into the lounge room, they will be offered sparkling wine by the two waitstaff, and as we discussed, a table will be set up against the wall with soft drinks, nibbles, and so on. Now, could we just go over the finger foods to give us both peace of mind?"

Carla was working hard to sound both professional and reassuring. It made a refreshing change from compiling shopping lists and arranging for pets to be cared for. She really wanted this to go well.

Greg had googled a recipe for Thai green curry and stopped off at the local deli to pick up any ingredients he thought they might be short of. Of course, he could have taken Davey and the ingredients to Betty's, but that would have involved a lot more hassle, and he wanted to spend some time with Davey that didn't appear contrived. In addition, he recalled the older two boys mentioning the resumption of hockey, and they usually had pies on such a night. An even more ominous plus was one that he hardly dared admit to himself.

"Your mum and I used to share cooking quite a lot in our early days," said Greg. "It's a nice thing to do together." The rice had been prepared, and under Greg's watchful eye, Davey was coating the chicken as per the instructions provided in the recipe. Greg was slicing and dicing as necessary. "You know, girls like it when you can cook, Davey. If you can cook *and* play guitar, I'd say you were well in!" Davey blushed.

"Plenty of time for that, though!" Greg joked, adopting a deep, gruff, seriously paternal tone as he unscrewed the cap from the olive oil. He began browning the meat in the pan and then passed the tongs to Davey, implying that he could take over the task. Watching Davey as he concentrated on turning the chicken, Greg made a conscious decision.

He was not moving anywhere.

"You remember Marinda, don't you?" Betty enquired as Helena loaded meat pies into the oven while Betty was making them both a cup of tea. Quite deftly, Helena observed.

"Marinda? Oh, yes. From your nursing days. Ran a health care centre or something similar? Lives in …"

"Northam," Betty filled in.

"Yes, Northam."

"I spoke to her on the phone today. Apparently two of her sons are doing some renovations to her house, rewiring, I think. Anyway, I suggested that she come here for a week. We haven't seen each other in ages. I thought it might be nice."

Helena shut the oven door with considerable force and attacked the dials irritably as she bemoaned the fact that she had forgotten to preheat it.

"Just where, exactly?"

"Where?"

"Whereabouts in the house will she sleep? It's a big house, yes, I accept that, but the boys hardly know her from Adam. Or Eve for that matter. Mum, really. What were you thinking?"

Betty looked completely taken aback.

Helena left the room and shut herself in the bathroom, where the tears flowed. She did her best to sob silently. Betty just wasn't aware of all the problems she was causing. Separated from Greg and Davey, not communicating effectively with Hugh and Louis (who seemed to want to be out most of the time), and being responsible for all the household duties was hard enough. Along with that, she was worrying about her mother's health as well as holding down a job. She jolted almost physically. Did her mother expect her to give up the job she loved and become a carer? Not only for her mother but also for whomever she chose to invite to stay?

She heard noisy scuffles and raised voices as the door clattered open and Hugh and Louis clambered in sharing a joke about their coach. Hastily she dried her eyes and began taking some deep breaths in an effort to pull herself together.

"Grandma—*Grandma*, what's wrong?" Helena heard Hugh's raised voice. "Louis, Ring Triple Zero!" he ordered. Helena burst out of the bathroom to see Hugh carefully but firmly lifting Betty up from the floor and easing her on to a chair. "I've got you; you're all right." Betty was holding a hand to her head.

"I've just bumped my head. I tried getting up too quickly. My own fault," she said, struggling for breath a little. Your mum ..."

"What? What happened!" yelled Helena as she stumbled into the kitchen and surveyed the scene.

"Mum," said Louis. "You look terrible."

"Is everything all right in here?" The voice trilled merrily through the chaos. It was Irene from next door. "I was just at the mailbox when I heard the commotion. Oh, Betty. Not a fall?"

"Thank you, Irene." Helena was regaining her composure. "Betty tried to get up too quickly and somehow bumped her head. I was in the bathroom." She wasn't going to expand on the whys and wherefores. "Mum, I don't think you need an ambulance. I'll take you to the hospital just to get you checked out. Cancel the ambulance, please, Louis. Well done, Hugh, for quick thinking." Louis replaced the receiver. He had been so overwhelmed with the speed of events that he hadn't actually gotten around to dialling the number.

"Well, if you're sure," said Irene. "I'll get out of your way, then." She was about to comment that Helena looked dreadful but felt it wise to simply return home.

"Thank you very much, Irene. We appreciate your kindness and your willingness to help." Helena smiled as broadly as she could manage in the circumstances. "I'll let you know tomorrow how it goes at the hospital." Irene nodded and made her retreat.

"Hugh, the pies will take a while, as I was late putting them in. I'll put through a call when I'm leaving the hospital. If your Dad phones, tell him I'll call later. Louis, please help me get Grandma Betty into the car."

All was silent in the car.

"Helena," began Betty as she somewhat awkwardly nursed a bruise on her head with an ice pack wrapped in a tea towel.

"I'm sorry for being short-tempered, Mum. I—"

"It's all right. Really. But I don't think I need to go to the hospital. I've just bumped my head, and to be honest, I think I bumped it on my stick as I tried to get up out of the chair too quickly. I didn't fall, because Hugh caught me. There's a late-night clinic at the local pharmacy. Can we go there? I'd much rather."

Helena was only half listening to Betty. Pleased with the boys' reactions earlier, she nonetheless regretted not being able to share in the Thai green curry as well as Davey's excitement about his first gig. In fact, she had to admit she felt resentful. Why was Greg …? Well, she didn't quite know what was going through his mind. *No, actually. You've left me.* Those words had stung. She had no choice. *Surely* he could see that.

CHAPTER 13

Mike felt a little uncomfortable knocking on the door to collect his father. Was he interfering? Did he have any right to question Jim's behaviour? He couldn't ask him straight out if he was *playing away*, so to speak. No more could he accuse him of reckless gambling with regard to his personal finances. The devious tactics employed by private eyes were totally alien to him, and his father was right. He didn't really like pubs.

Jim, however, answered the door in quite a breezy fashion, bidding a cheery farewell to Mary and wishing her happy viewing. (*"Sleepless in Seattle,"* he informed Mike. "She loves it.")

"I haven't enjoyed a pint in a while," Jim commented, winking at Mike as if they were about to embark on some kind of dubious enterprise. They discussed the current controversy over teachers' wages that had featured on the news. They were both interested, as Sarah was soon to complete her teaching degree and take her place in the world of education.

"What a lot of cars!" Mike said as he approached the parking lot at the front of the pub.

"I'll say," agreed Jim. "There's a good one, though."

Mike pulled in to the spot, and they both got out of the car and walked towards the pub entrance. It was then that they saw the billboard.

"Oh …" said Jim delightedly. "It's a quiz night! I haven't been to a quiz night in years!"

"Me neither," said Mike as his heart sank. A quiet man-to-man talk was not going to work alongside several rowdy teams of trivia buffs vying for a place in the final. "I didn't know you liked quiz nights."

"I didn't know you liked pubs," said Jim as he punched Mike playfully on the arm. A puzzled look crossed Mike's face. Something was definitely up with his father.

Betty was given the once-over by a nurse at the clinic, who felt sure that she had simply made a hasty wrong move and managed somehow to clout herself with her own stick. Helena had agreed to take Betty to the clinic with the understanding that she would go to the hospital if advised to do so. There was a bit of a bump and a bruise but no dizziness or disorientation. Some arnica and an aspirin should see her right.

"I am so sorry, Helena."

"You don't have to apologise, Mum. It was my fault. I'm a little tired ..."

"But that's just it, darling girl." Betty hadn't used that term in ages. "It's not your fault. None of this is your fault. But that isn't really what I meant. About Marinda ..."

"Yes, yes," Helena interrupted. "Of course. It's your house. You can choose to have anyone you like to stay."

"Yes, but the thought behind it was that if Marinda is there, well, you and the boys don't need to be."

Helena pulled up at the lights and looked across at her mother.

"You could go home. You need to go home."

Jim had approached a friendly-looking member of one of the pub trivia teams and asked for a couple of sheets of paper from his yellow notepad. Mike had reluctantly agreed to partake in the quiz with his father, but merely as observers. They would jot down the answers to achieve their own private score. Mike acknowledged that there would be no chance of any meaningful conversation so he may as well go with the flow. Jim didn't appear to take much notice of any of the pretty girls dotted around the crowd. Admittedly, they were young. But there were two barmaids considerably more advanced in years working behind the bar. Jim didn't seem interested in them either. Mike had never considered Jim to be a philanderer. As for the possibility of gambling … Dealing with stocks and shares for years as he had, maybe he was missing the thrill and excitement. To be frank, he didn't even know whether Jim took part in the lottery or not.

"Raffle tickets for you two gentlemen?" A rather well-endowed bottle blonde leant forward enticingly towards both Mike and Jim, displaying her wares. "All in a good cause," she said with a grin.

"No, thanks," said Jim. "Oh, unless you …?" He addressed Mike as an afterthought.

"No. Thank you. We aren't sure how long we shall stay." Probably not gambling, then. "I'll get the first round."

"If you put as much as possible away when you dry it, you mostly save yourself a job," Greg advised Davey as he added a little more washing-up liquid to the hot water before tackling the wok. "You know where it goes, and if you don't, it shouldn't be difficult to work out." Davey had enjoyed making the curry alongside his dad. "Have you worked out what you're wearing for your gig? You need to get that sorted well before time."

"My black jeans are smart," Davey answered, "and I've got a plain black T-shirt."

"I think a proper shirt would be better. It doesn't have to be expensive. Would you have enough in your allowance if we paid half?"

"Thanks, Dad." Davey was genuinely chuffed. "Tailors are open until nine—shall I take a bike ride?"

"I'll come with you for a second opinion. If you are serious about this, then start as you mean to go on. People are paying you money. They have a right to expect that you will look the part, be fully prepared, and behave professionally."

Louis and Hugh were watching a documentary about the future of space travel, leaving Helena and Betty alone in the kitchen with coffee to chat following their recent ordeal. They were seated on a small sofa that sat in a recess created by a bay window overlooking the garden.

"You're sure about this then, Mum?"

"I'm as sure as I can be, love. One thing I am certain about is that nobody, and I mean *nobody*, is happy at the moment. You know that too, really. This past week has been miserable. Go home, take the boys, spend quality time with that lovely man of yours, and forget about me for a week at least. Marinda is eminently capable, and we genuinely want to spend time together."

"But it can't be a long-term solution, though, can it?" persisted Helena.

"No, but let's not think long term right now. Marinda should be here tomorrow mid-afternoon. If you and the boys pack up tonight, you can return home after work. Let the boys know and phone Greg, eh?"

Greg and Davey had found a smart-looking shirt that was mostly black apart from a delicate white-and-grey pinstripe and a grey collar. In the same store, there was a rack of reduced dress pants. Davey tried a black pair on with the shirt and agreed with his dad that the resultant look was superior to one that featured black jeans, but he would need dress shoes to carry off the whole ensemble.

"The shoes can be part of your birthday present. It's only a month away." Greg was impressed with how good Davey looked. Appearing older than his current fifteen years and giving off an air of confidence, he presented well. And Greg was sure that he certainly had the musical skills to succeed.

"I can't wait to show Mum," he said, reverting to his boyish demeanour and reminding Greg that despite the clothes and the talent, he still needed a lot of support and encouragement.

CHAPTER 14

"Ah ... Helena." Gina was genuinely pleased to see Helena and felt she looked more like her usual self. "How is everything?"

"We're getting there," Helena replied. "I've got a bit of a reprieve, as Mum has a friend staying for a week," she said, taking her place behind her desk and booting up her laptop.

"Good. Make the most of it, then." Gina turned to the glassed entrance as a tall gentleman wearing a worn yet prestigious school scarf came through into the foyer. The weather didn't warrant a scarf—a hint of intimidation, maybe? "Mr. Roberts, good morning. I was expecting you. Please come through to my office," she said, leading the way.

Helena felt bad that she had used the word *reprieve*. It sounded as if she'd been let out of prison. What made it even worse was that she *felt* as if she'd been let out of prison. Entering her password, Helena clicked on to the overview of the day's events: an excursion for the Year 8 students and a fire drill. Nothing that should set the alarms bells ringing. She smiled to herself at her own pun.

Jeannie and Josie were standing at the end of a line of students, awaiting the somewhat dubious honour of being inoculated by the health centre nurse. Cecily joined them.

"It's a pain, this, innit?"

"Well, I guess it's better than not," smiled Josie encouragingly. Cecily looked a little pale.

"I hate needles." Cecily stuck her hands in her pockets. "Got a good weekend lined up?"

"Well, we're both waiting drinks and party food for my mum," said Jeannie. "Not much apart from that. You?"

"Oh yeah, I remember you sayin'." Cecily eyed the head of the queue nervously. "No. My mum, well, stepmum, well, my Dad's girlfriend, has choofed off somewhere, so I might just keep him company. Watch a movie or whatever." Cecily scuffed her feet. "He's all right, my Dad. Always tellin' me to *make the most of my opportunities*." She looked down at her feet again. "Dunno where the opportunities are meant to come from, though."

The queue moved along a little. "Nearly your turn." Cecily grinned at Josie.

Carla was attending to her paperwork a day early in order to be completely free on Saturday. She had reason enough to feel pleased with how far her business had come, seeing as she had just started with herself doing odd jobs for people. Her current list of clients, along with any potential newcomers, needed to be adequately maintained and valued. Yesterday she had been asked if she could organise a house-sitter for a month. A middle-aged couple had booked an overseas trip to see their brand-new granddaughter in America. They wanted their house to look lived in, but even more importantly, they wanted the two small dogs they doted on to remain in familiar surroundings and be fed and exercised. They also had created a rather splendid patio area complete with several large potted ferns.

Mrs. Young's party could herald a whole new line of work. (She supposed she should refer to the function as Mr. and Mrs. Young's party, but thinking about it, she couldn't recall Mr. Young even getting a mention in any of her talks with Mrs. Young.) Plans for the event loomed large, and she had checked her preparation list several times. She didn't have any huge areas of concern, although she hoped she hadn't asked too much of Davey.

There was backup music just in case, she reminded herself. Also, she had little knowledge of what was happening with the finger foods, other than being assured everything was well and truly in hand in that department.

"I'm picking up a headache, I think," Josie remarked to Jeannie over lunch. "I don't feel like eating."

Jeannie noticed that she looked flushed and her neck had started to look a bit blotchy. "Perhaps you should get a slip for the nurse," she suggested.

"No. They'll phone Mum at work. And we've got double art."

By mid-afternoon, however, Josie looked awful. Her eyes were red and puffy, and the blotches right around her neck looked worse. So much so that Mr. Burgess issued her with a note for the nurse and insisted that she go straight to the sickroom. Her mother was sent for, and the nurse advised that she be taken to the doctor, especially bearing in mind that they had been given inoculations that morning.

Cecily wrote down a phone number on a scrap of paper she had torn from her student diary and handed it to Jeannie. "Just in case you need someone to fill in."

Helena took in the animated conversation going on between all three of her sons on the return journey home. Their hastily repacked cases had been bundled into the boot. Louis had requested fish and chips for tea, claiming that having dinner together again was reason enough. It struck Helena that regardless of motivation, it was pleasing to hear Louis propose a family-centred cause.

Hugh was asking questions of Davey with regard to his forthcoming gig in a way that showed genuine interest, and she herself felt that her world, for a short time at least, was once again finding an even keel.

"Of course I understand, Louise," said a concerned Carla into the phone. "I'm just pleased to hear that an allergic reaction is all it is and that it should be cleared up in a few days. Don't give it a second thought, please. I'll work something out easily enough. Bye for now and take care."

"Well, problem number one!" Carla said in a jocular tone that didn't quite match up to how she felt. Mentally she was going through her staff list, wondering who could step in at short notice.

"Um, I've got this number," Jeannie offered, handing her mother the hastily scrawled note that Cecily had supplied her with. "It's Cecily. I don't know her well because she hasn't been in the area long. She's not really my type, but ..."

"This is important, Jeannie. I need to be able to trust whomever I employ."

"I know that Mum, but today I kind of felt a bit sorry for her, you know? It's like she needs someone on her side. I can keep an eye on her, and you'll be there too, won't you?" Jeannie couldn't see a huge problem. They were only handing out drinks and bits of food after all. "How about I ring and then pass her on to you? You can sort of make it sound like a serious interview."

Jeannie called and, to her surprise, found herself talking to Cecily's father. She briefly explained who she was and what she wanted.

"Can I speak to your mother, please?" he asked. A nonplussed Jeannie handed the phone to Carla and was intrigued to see her mother caught a little on the back foot. Mr. Reid wanted to know exactly what was required from Cecily.

"OK then," he said. "It will be up to her."

Carla waited for Cecily to take the phone and realised that it was in fact Cecily's father who had been conducting the interview. She explained the requirements to Cecily and offered her the job.

The Young family was one of those entities that caused people to feel a little uneasy. They were nice enough people, but they almost seemed to personify characters pictured on the cover of an old-fashioned children's storybook. Mrs. Young undoubtedly was in charge of the household, not with an iron fist but with a diligence akin to the persuasive smoothing of a steam iron. Mr. Young applied himself to his work as a bank manager happily enough because he could not contemplate doing anything else. He had hoped for sons and had been slightly disappointed with two girls, although he would never have admitted that to a soul. The two girls fell into compliant line with their mother's wishes in just about everything and eventually married two brothers. They, in turn, each provided Mr. and Mrs. Young with a grandson, much to the delight of Mr. Young.

It was for the sake of his two grandsons that Kenneth had been ensconced in his workshop for several recent weeks. He had purchased from a former work colleague a large electric racing car circuit, complete with all the accoutrements, for a most reasonable price. It needed work, as it had remained stored and unused for several years. Kenneth held visions of himself and his grandsons waving chequered flags and communicating in racing circuit banter with enthusiastic fervour. The extensive looped track required a good deal of room, so he had moved and rearranged various items of unused furniture and so on to make the most of the space. Maureen showed little interest in anything to do with the workshop—apart from utilising the fridge and freezer for whenever she made the most of frozen specials at the supermarket or needed to store drinks in readiness for Christmas celebrations and the like. Currently, of course, the appliances were crammed with the finger foods lovingly prepared by herself and her two daughters for the upcoming anniversary party.

Jim persuaded Mary to ring through to Mike and Lizzie and invite them to dinner on Saturday night. He could not shake the feeling that something was not quite the ticket. Mike and Lizzie had made big sacrifices to see him and Mary right after the appalling mess he had gotten them into. He owed it to them to help them in any way he could.

Mary, in turn, was worried that Mike might reveal that she was the one who had contacted him because of her concerns for Jim.

"Yes, of course we can come to dinner. That would be lovely. Sarah will be here, though, as she has a big assignment due." Lizzie was pleased that Mike might have a second opportunity to speak to Jim.

"Oh, that makes it even more special. She can come?"

"Even students have to eat!" laughed Lizzie.

CHAPTER 15

Maureen Young awoke from her slumber at around seven in the morning, as she knew she would. She had gone to bed at eleven the night before, full of joyful anticipation about the forthcoming party the next day, having taken a sleeping pill to ensure a good night's sleep. Sliding into slippers and a dressing gown, she checked on the recently acquired and carefully chosen dress that hung proudly in the walk-in robe. Perfect.

She made her way towards the room occupied by Kenneth. They had mutually decided once the girls left home that they had no further need for *that type of thing*. To be frank, Kenneth was almost relieved. After the first flushes and rushes of their week-long honeymoon on Rottnest Island, providing intimate satisfaction for his spouse had become somewhat of a chore to him.

Maureen had reserved the task of purchasing and installing fairy lights around the garden for her husband. It would keep him well occupied and leave her free to supervise or contend with any last-minute details that might arise. Maureen had ensured that the exact style of garden lighting she required to create the desired effect was in plentiful supply at the DIY franchise store a twenty-minute drive away. She would serve them both cereal and then write down a list for him before getting ready for the hairdressing appointments she had made for her and her two daughters.

Surprised to find the door open and the bed unmade, she continued on towards the kitchen. The bottom drawer of one of the cupboards beneath the kitchen bench appeared to have been ransacked. It usually contained the varied collection of bin liners, sandwich bags, and rolls of plastic wrap associated with everyday food preservation. Some remained in the drawer; however, the floor was littered with the remains of half-torn-off liners and numerous unused bags.

"Kenneth?" she called. "Where are you? What's happened here?" On hearing no response, she began clearing up the detritus. He couldn't be far away. He'd probably gone out for a paper, although he'd not have much chance to read it today, she thought wryly. What on earth had he been looking for in the drawer? She put the kettle on but then decided she would shower early. Then by the time he returned, she could start work on the list and have his full attention.

Dressing comfortably in a skirt and matching top, Maureen was pleased to hear Ben's car pull up onto the driveway. She mentally congratulated herself on hiring Carla. She had been a godsend—an expensive godsend, but a godsend nonetheless. She peeked out of the window to see him move to the back of the vehicle, presumably to unload the pots of colour that were to adorn the front steps. She hadn't heard Kenneth return yet. A thought suddenly occurred to her. Maybe he was preparing some sort of special surprise. Not pink flamingos surely. A ruby wedding gift, perhaps? It was unlike him, but …

Maureen served herself a bowl of cereal. Their hair appointments were booked for ten that morning. The first job upon returning from the hairdresser would be to wash all the glasses. They were stored in the workshop in cardboard boxes. Maybe she would fetch them into the kitchen in readiness. Once the glasses were washed, she would remove all the finger foods from the freezer.

Once again, she was surprised at finding the workshop roller door raised. "Kenneth? Are you in here?" She stood stock-still and stared. Her mouth dropped open as she took in the sight before her. The fridge and freezer doors were both wide open, and dumped in front of them, languishing in a large puddle of water, were several black bin liners that appeared to have been hastily stuffed with the entire contents of the freezer. All the prepared finger food lay in half-defrosted congealed masses of inedible matter. Her hands went to her mouth, and her heart lurched. "Kenneth! *Kenneth!* Oh my *God—Kenneth!*" She ran around to the front of the house in an absolute panic, with her hands raised to the heavens. In shock, Ben almost dropped the box of plant pots he was carrying.

"What's the matter, Mrs. Young. Is someone …?" He put down the box he was carrying, and Maureen grabbed hold of his arms and stared at him like a maniac. Seemingly incapable of speech, she almost dragged him around to the back of the house in the direction of the workshop. Ben was more than half expecting to find a body swinging from the rafters. Maureen stared back and forth from the freezer mess to Ben helplessly several times. Ben gathered that the party food was obviously no longer fit for human consumption, but beyond that, he felt somewhat inadequately prepared to deal with a woman about to pass out with apoplexy.

"Is your husband …?"

"I don't know *where* he is!" she wailed.

Ben pulled a mobile phone out of his pocket and phoned Carla. He outlined a brief description of the crisis to his mother, handed the phone to Maureen, and indicated to her via hand signals that he would get back to the work he had come for.

"Problem number two," Carla muttered to herself as she took a fairly brisk walk around to the rear entrance of Mike and Lizzie's place She had waved off the three guys on their way to their usual game. Mike had offered to stay in case he could help, but Carla felt sure she would get female assistance fairly easily.

"Can I come in?" she asked, rapping her knuckles on the kitchen door and opening it without actually entering. "Helena! Oh …" Helena stood, and they embraced.

"Carlz … I thought I'd best leave you alone today, what with your big party and all."

"Well, that's why I'm here." She looked at both of them with deliberately pleading eyes.

"Sit down, then. Coffee?" offered Lizzie.

"Thanks. You wouldn't believe it. It's like the classic 'What could possibly go wrong for a party of sixty-plus people that's meant to be happening in about eight hours?'"

"No food?" Lizzie suggested, eyebrows arched in irony.

"Exactly!"

"*No!*" they chorused.

"I was joking!" said Lizzie. "Don't tell me the freezer got turned off …"

"The freezer got turned off!"

"No."

"Seriously," said Carla. "I've just got off the phone from Mrs. Young, who is totally and utterly beside herself. Plus her husband has gone missing … She thinks he might be buying her a present or something. I told her to ask Ben to help her clear away the mess and then go to the hairdresser as planned and I would come up with something." Her eyes clouded, but she would not give in to tears. It had to be dealt with efficiently. "Help," she begged.

Ben told Mrs. Young that he would be happy to clear away the rotting food and suggested that she get to the hairdresser on time. Bewailing the fact that the installation of fairy lights might not happen if Mr. Young did not return almost immediately, Ben suggested that he phone through to Carla for approval of the extra time (indicating that he wasn't prepared to do it for free) and take on the task. He would know what was required, he assured her. Ben actually thought it would be best for Mr. Young if he was discovered diligently assisting with the mood lighting on her return. Murdering him would mess up her hair.

Sarah arrived to find the three women making a list of sweet and savoury finger foods. Carla briefly explained the problem. Sarah listened and wished them all a well-intended "Good luck with that!" She then excused herself, as she had to get her head around her impending assignment.

"Oh, I saw you in town the other day. I thought we could share a cuppa, but then I lost you."

"No, it couldn't have been me. I don't usually go into town during the week. I'll leave you to get on."

"Coffee before you start?" asked Lizzie.

"I'll make myself one a bit later. Thanks, Mum."

They were all familiar with a local delicatessen store that was well stocked with specialist items of the type they needed. There was no time to waste, which was why they were working out a menu and writing a list before setting off.

"What have we got so far?" asked Helena.

Carla read the list aloud. "Plain crackers with brie and sun-dried tomatoes, chilli crackers with cream cheese and cucumber, both red and green cocktail onions, chorizo, pineapple on cocktail sticks, creamed corn mini quiches, mini french toast with sardines ..." She paused to take a breath before continuing. "Rough mini chunks of french bread with tabbouleh dip and smoked salmon dip, papa Italiana cocktail sausage rolls, mini choux pastry eclairs, strawberries dipped in chocolate on cocktail sticks, mini pastry cases with chocolate mousse, white flaked chocolate and almond slivers, and mini pastry cases with lemon custard and glazed mandarin segments. We'll also have Turkish delight squares, mini macarons, and mini coffee crème biscuits. The celebration cupcakes are being delivered in the afternoon. Forty to create the centrepiece and an additional twenty five to make up the full complement," Carla added.

"Sounds good to me," said Lizzie. "Should we get cracking, then?"

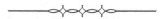

When she met them at the hairdressers, Maureen Young decided not to mention to her daughters that her husband of forty years was absent and unaccounted for. She attended Hairwaves regularly, so the apprentice washing her hair was asking politely about the party arrangements. The same junior sat her down comfortably with a pile of magazines and asked if she would like her usual coffee. Maureen demurred, making the excuse of having an extra cup at breakfast that morning. In fact, she was feeling quite sick in her stomach. She would strangle Kenneth when he got home. She picked up a magazine. It promised to reveal the real reason behind Brad and Angelina's marital breakdown, which of course did nothing to ease her current level of stress. *Bloody men*, she thought.

"So, Maureen," said her regular stylist brightly as she removed the towel from Maureen's head, "everything ready? No disasters?"

"No. All going to plan." Where the hell was Kenneth?

CHAPTER 16

Hugh was pleased to be home. He had thought that staying at Grandma Betty's would be all right, and it was all right, but not *quite* right. Mum seemed stressed out all the time, resulting in a rather tense atmosphere. The house itself, whilst spacious, didn't altogether fit somehow. Louis liked playing ping-pong and asked Hugh to play repeatedly, which got on his nerves a bit. Hugh was in fact impressed with Davey. That cool no-uniform stunt was awesome, and taking on a musical gig was brave. He could see that. Everyone knew Davey played well, but playing in public was something else.

Hugh knocked tentatively on the door of number 25, and Jeannie answered. She immediately reprimanded herself for having a lazy morning. Mum was next door, Dad was at golf, and she had answered the door in her PJs.

"Oh. Hi, Hugh. I'm sorry. I've been … Sorry. Come in."

"Shall I come back later? I just wondered if you could help me with something."

For the past six months, Jeannie had lived in hope that Hugh would show some kind of interest in her. It seemed unbelievable that he should be standing on the doorstep asking for her help when she was dressed in PJs, looking like a dorky twelve-year-old.

Hugh briefly outlined what he had in mind. Frankly, she wouldn't have cared if he had asked her to help unblock the loo.

She asked if he could give her ten minutes and she would come around to his place.

Davey was nervous but relatively calm. He knew he should do some guitar practise, but not too much. Probably doing something physical would be sensible. He decided to go for a swim at the local pool. It was about a twenty-five-minute walk each way. What with the walk and the swim, he would be exercising for a couple of hours. He was finding his gear and a towel when he heard a knock at the door.

"That's for me, I think," called Hugh as he passed Davey rolling up his togs in the largest towel he could find.

It was Jeannie. Davey's heart plummeted. Jeannie—for Hugh. No one spoke for a moment.

"Are you going for a swim?" asked Hugh a little lamely.

"I thought I'd do some exercise."

"Good idea. We'll see you later, then."

"I guess this wasn't what either of you two had in mind," said Carla as Lizzie backed out of the driveway. "I can't tell you how grateful I am. I owe you both big time!"

"I'm just so glad to be home," Helena said. "Helping you out assuages the guilt."

"Guilt?" repeated Carla. "Helena. You've just spent more than a week with your mother, been away from Greg and Davey, coped with Hugh and Louis being removed from home … What on earth have you got to feel guilty about?"

Carla's phone rang. It was Ben. "The mess is cleared away; I've got all the lights, and I'm about to start putting them up."

"Great," said Carla. "Well done."

"It's weird, though. There's no sign of Mr. Young. Isn't this an anniversary?"

"I know. I'll talk to Mrs. Young in an hour or so. If he is buying a present, he'd better make it a hum-dinger. I wouldn't want to cross Mrs. Young when she's got her gander up!"

"Should someone check the hospitals or something?"

"Not yet … and not us. A family member should do it. But hopefully he'll turn up soon. Fingers crossed."

"Carla, sorry, but I'm not too familiar with the quickest route to this place. I have to check every time. Could you look it up on the phone for me?" Lizzie had just pulled up at the lights.

Carla bade a hasty farewell and began typing the store name into the maps app.

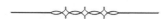

Mrs. Young was pleased with the finished look. She had been coloured, highlighted, trimmed, and blow-dried. Her daughters had both been straightened. Whilst not being entirely sure that long hair suited any woman over thirty, she had to admit they did look quite lovely. The three of them confirmed with each other a confluence at 6:00 p.m., just in case any last-minute problems should arise. They went their separate ways. Maureen had not mentioned her errant husband. She was about to turn on the engine when her phone rang.

"Ben here, Mrs. Young. The lights are up, I've given them a test, and they look great. The entry looks stunning too. There's nothing else you need me for?"

"No. Thank you so much, Ben. My husband is there by now, I suppose?"

"No, but remember traffic can be bad on a Saturday …" It was all he could think of by way of sensitive counsel.

The delicatessen lived up to its reputation and was able to supply everything on Carla's list. They also purchased some sushi rolls and slabs of soft nougat. Lizzie had a rather small car boot, so some of the purchases had to sit beside Helena for the return journey.

"Thank you so much, Carlz, for the opportunity you've given Davey. He is so thrilled."

"It's my pleasure. I thought of him immediately. I just hope he doesn't feel under too much pressure. I mean, he's young … But there is backup just in case." Lizzie slowed at the yellow detour sign. "Struth. Roadworks. I hate detours. Why on a Saturday?" As they approached the intersection, however, they saw a huge spillage of mulch along with a large overturned trailer blocking the entire roadway.

"I do hope Mr. Young has turned up by now," said Carla thoughtfully.

"Yes. With the mother of all gifts!" laughed Lizzie.

"What could it be, do you think?" Helena mused aloud.

"A partridge in a bloody pear tree, perhaps?" said Lizzie. "She'll be knocked sideways!"

"I think *he* might be the one who is knocked sideways," Carla countered.

Davey was glad for the time to think. He was aware of the chick attraction of his older brother, good-looking, fit, clever, and a genuinely nice guy. Yet he possessed that something that prevented the *nice guy* persona from making him appear weak or feeble. It was obvious that Jeannie might well fall for him. He hadn't really considered it before because the six children from the three families had grown up together almost like brothers and sisters. Jeannie was a year older than Davey, but only in school years. The age difference was about eight months. That didn't matter surely? Jeannie appreciated his musical talent; he was certain of that. He was also sure that Jeannie really liked him. But there was like and *like*. Between himself and Hugh, there probably wasn't much competition.

During his swim, he just did straight laps and went over his repertoire in his head. He had found an old book of folk songs in a music shop bargain basket about a year ago. He had taken each melody, learnt it, and then improvised until the original tune almost disappeared into the background and became a golden thread woven between harmonic notes to create a musical tapestry. Sometimes he composed his own melodies. He had plenty of material, and he could easily play repeats because he wasn't giving a concert.

The walk home buoyed his spirits further—until he turned into Capstan Court. The trio of houses at the base of the cul-de-sac was a fair distance away but clearly in view. Davey saw two figures walking from the doorway at the side of the house around to the front driveway. They were chatting together like good friends. It was Hugh and Jeannie. Davey stopped walking towards the house and pulled himself behind a large shrub growing in a rather unruly fashion at the head of one of the gardens in the court. Then Davey saw Hugh's outstretched hand take hold of Jeannie's and twirl her in towards him as if they were performing a dance. Jeannie threw her head back and laughed. Davey froze as he saw Jeannie lay her head on Hugh's shoulder for a moment and then look up at him expectantly. He couldn't bear to watch, yet he couldn't take his eyes off them. *Don't*, he begged silently. *Please, don't.*

The detour added about fifteen minutes to the return journey for the three friends. They had lots to talk about, so they were hardly aware of time passing. Helena had suggested that they should perhaps drop the food off on their way back. Mrs. Young would know the catering problem had been solved at least. They agreed that Helena and Lizzie would take the food through; it would take a few trips from car to kitchen. Carla would be free to have a chat with Mrs. Young regarding her husband.

"I don't want to think the worst, Mrs. Young, but have you considered calling the local hospitals?"

"He's not in hospital, I'm sure," responded Maureen." He's taken his wallet. It's got his driving licence in it."

Carla presumed Mrs. Young to mean a hospital staff member would phone *her*, should the need arise.

Carla spoke gently and quietly. "Maureen, are you sure that you want to go ahead with this party? If the money ..."

"I am *not* cancelling this party, Carla. Over sixty people will arrive at this house at seven o'clock this evening, and *a party they shall have!*" Maureen's face was red and defiant. "He has to come back. He simply *has* to."

Carla nodded dubiously. "Was everything all right last night when you both went to bed?"

"Yes. Of course it was. I think he was playing around with those stupid racing cars. Men can be so infantile." She glanced briefly at Carla, then looked away. "Thank you for the finger foods. They'll be second best, of course. I appreciate your coming to the rescue. I'll start putting them all together and box them up so they are ready to go onto serving platters tonight."

"If you're sure," said Carla, beginning to make her exit. "I'll see you at six thirty, then."

Back in the car, Carla did make phone calls to the two local hospitals. There was no evidence of a husband missing in action. *Please let him show up soon,* she willed silently.

CHAPTER 17

Betty couldn't remember the last time she'd had this much fun. Marinda had caught a taxi from the bus terminal to Betty's place. As well as the usual luggage of clothing and ablution gear expected for a week- long stay, Marinda had raided her local charity store for all sorts of things designed to add a little sparkle to their time together. A giant floor puzzle suitable for seven-year-olds was spread out over the ping-pong table for them to work on whenever they wanted to. Three movie collections featuring Fred Astaire, Cary Grant, and Goldie Hawn were placed on the unit that housed a (thankfully) big-screen television. Two large print volumes, one of crosswords and one of quiz questions, went on the coffee table. To top it all off, Marinda had crammed jam, cream, and all the ingredients necessary for baking several batches of scones into an esky. Afternoon tea was a must, she insisted. Did Betty have leaf tea and a teapot? It was far superior to teabags.

Carla was seriously concerned. Had she bitten off more than she could chew? This was a first-time event plan, and she had chosen to use an inexperienced musician and an untried waitperson. She had taken on the catering requirements at the last minute and was dealing with a client who seemed to be close to a nervous breakdown. She refused to admit to anybody that her husband of forty years might have just upped and left her on the day of their ruby wedding party, organised to celebrate a supposedly joyous occasion with more than sixty people.

She was lying on their bed. Douglas had plumped up the pillows and was sitting next to her with his shoeless feet on the blue-and-white duvet cover that Carla loved.

"To be honest, I think any first time event would seem stressful. There's a big difference between arranging for someone to walk a dog and overseeing a party for sixty odd people. He laughed. 'Odd' being an apt description of Mr. and Mrs. Young, by the sounds of it." Carla didn't respond. "You've done all you can. Booking Davey was a great idea, and you have a backup plan if he loses it. You have a replacement at short notice for Josie, and because Jeannie knows her, she should be OK showing her the ropes. The food is delivered. If you are serious about going down the event coordinator path, then these kinds of stresses are part of the whole deal. You're a born organiser, sweetheart. Chalk it up to experience." Douglas leaned over and kissed her.

"Thanks. I love you." Carla laced her fingers around the back of his neck and kissed him in return. "I agree with all of that, but what about the missing husband? Is she really going to welcome all these guests and field any questions as to his whereabouts?"

"I really don't know. But you've got no control over that. Let's just hope that by the time you get there tonight, he'll have turned up."

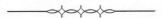

Greg was almost euphoric. The three guys had enjoyed their game of golf and followed it up with two rounds at the bar. Currently (though he could hardly believe it himself), all five family members were tidying up the front garden. He had persuaded the three boys to give him half an hour. "That's two and a half hours of gardening. Ben worked hard to make it look good. Let's keep it up."

When the shed project was going on, Hugh had set aside one large plastic tub for them to put any small gardening items in so long as they were in good nick. Odd gloves and tools were located all over the place. When they were collected together, there proved to be enough gloves for one pair each (not necessarily matching) and some kind of implement. Greg designated everyone an area to work on, and they were all busy. Feeling as if he deserved a father of the year award, he himself was removing a few weeds that had sprouted around the For Sale sign. He wanted to rip up the sign and set fire to it. A pang of guilt ran through him. He hadn't told Helena of his resolve to remain in the house they both loved. He would tell her tonight.

"That's the landline," said Helena. "I'll go." She returned a few minutes later. "It was the agent," she said, squeezing her hands back into a pair of gloves that were a size too small. "Good news," she said. "We've got an offer on the house. I said you'll call back in about half an hour."

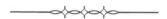

Cecily arrived just after six o'clock. "I'm a bit early. Hope that's all right. The next bus would have got me here a bit late."

Jeannie had answered the door. "I didn't realise you were coming by bus. You should have said. We would have arranged a pickup. We'll definitely see you home safely."

"Good, thanks. Dad was a bit worried about that."

Jeannie wondered why her dad wasn't driving her. She took in what Cecily was wearing. She had complied with the black; however, *tart* rather than *smart* was the general impression. Her skirt was too short, and her top was too low. Mum wouldn't be pleased. "I'm about to get changed. Come with me, and we can chat." Jeannie led the way to her room and began assembling items together from her wardrobe. She put on black dress pants, a black shirt with a collar, and finished it off with a black sleeveless vest. Retrieving a pair of black patent flatties from the back of the robe, she slid them on and crossed to the shelf below her mirror to fetch her hairbrush. As she began brushing vigorously, Cecily considered the way Jeannie looked and then looked in the long mirror on the wardrobe door. "Is this all right?" she asked. "I haven't got much black stuff. Dad doesn't like me wearing a lot of black."

Jeannie didn't quite know what to make of Cecily. She was usually brash and appeared nonconformist, but she obviously took notice of her

dad. "Um, maybe you could put these leggings on under your skirt."
Jeannie wondered if Cecily would tell her to get stuffed, but she meekly
took the leggings from Jeannie and pulled them on. "That's good. I've
got a lacy stretch sleeveless top somewhere …" She rummaged about in
a drawer. "Here. Try that over the top you've got on." Cecily did as was
requested and smiled at her reflection.

"I look nearly as posh as you!"

"You said you'd done a bit of waitressing. Whereabouts?"

Cecily looked rather sheepish. "I sort of have." A pause hung in
the air. Jeannie looked directly into Cecily's eyes and made it clear she
expected an answer. "I've helped out in Roma's chippie van a couple of
times." Cecily looked away. "I really wanna do this, Jeannie."

"Who's Roma?"

"Dad's girlfriend."

Jeannie nodded. "Look, Cecily, this job is really important to
Mum. She's been asked to supply waiting staff before, but this party is
something else. I've stuck my neck out in recommending you. Please
don't let Mum down."

Cecily smiled. "Your mum will think I'm Bindi friggin' Irwin. So
long as I don't open my mouth!"

They both laughed. Jeannie offered up a silent prayer to whoever
might be inclined to listen.

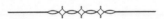

Carla opened the door to Davey. "Very smart," she commented.
"Have you double-checked you've got everything?"

"Only about six times." Davey grinned. Carla realised how young
he looked when he smiled. Jeannie and Cecily came through from the
bedroom. Jeannie was carrying an A4 document wallet in her hand.

"Is Hugh with you, Davey?"

"No. Why should he be?" He was rattled. As if the kiss wasn't enough.

At that moment, Hugh rapped on the door and Carla let him in.
The entry was getting a little crowded. Hugh looked directly at Jeannie,
and she gave a nod.

"We had this idea," said Hugh. Jeannie passed the A4 wallet to Davey. He opened it and removed the contents. There was a laminated sheet of white card inside. It had a black-edged border about a centimetre from the edge on all four sides. Left of centre, in black Broadway font, was his name: Davey Browne. Underneath that was a single silver line and beneath that the words Classical Guitar Ambience Music, followed by a telephone number.

In addition, there were a dozen small cards, printed the same but with a picture of a guitar on the back.

"Sorry there are only twelve cards. We ran out. Break a leg, bro."

Approaching the Young's home, Carla's attention was drawn to the lighting. It was effective even though there was a while to go before darkness. She deliberately didn't pull up on the driveway but parked in front of a wide walkway that led through to a children's playground. Davey was retrieving his guitar from the boot. Jeannie gave him a hand with his music stand and music case. Cecily picked up a box with kitchen paraphernalia that Carla had thought might be needed. Carla remained unencumbered apart from her handbag, which included her phone as well as the usual items she carried.

One of Mrs. Young's daughters, whom she had met once very briefly, walked towards the car with hands outstretched in greeting. "I've been watching out for you," she said. "I'm Glenda."

"Yes, I remember," said Carla.

"Mother asked me to tell you that Father has gone out to buy more alcohol, as he was worried we might be a little short, and she asked if you would go see her as soon as you arrive. She's in the study writing a few thank-you cards."

Carla breathed a huge sigh of relief. No doubt she would hear from Maureen a somewhat doctored tale of Kenneth's exploits.

CHAPTER 18

Carla had instructed Davey to play some recorded music as soon as possible. If there was music playing already, he would feel calmer setting up. Jeannie and Cecily were dispatched to the kitchen to ensure that the first two drinks trays were ready and to see if they could do anything to help. She made her way to the study, knocked, and walked in. Maureen Young was indeed sitting at a desk writing some thank-you cards.

"You look lovely, Maureen. I'm so relieved to hear that your husband …" Maureen held up one hand and put the fingers of her other hand to her lips. Carla said nothing.

"Shh. Strictly speaking, Mr. Young, Kenneth, isn't here at the moment."

"Strictly speaking?"

"He phoned Glenda and told her he was buying drinks." Maureen was hastily stuffing cards into envelopes and scrawling names on the front.

"I see," said Carla, not seeing at all.

"We've plenty of alcohol for drinks, so I don't know why he's panicking." Maureen collected the cards together in one pile and tapped them neatly on the desk before placing them by the phone. "I'll remember they are there," she said. "So everything can go ahead as planned. Shall we go through to the kitchen? I didn't thank you properly for the food. It all looks so nice."

Carla followed Mrs. Young through to the kitchen. The savoury finger food was laid out on platters, and it did look perfectly presentable. Cecily and Jeannie were pouring sparkling wine into flutes. She decided to check on Davey.

So had Mr. Young returned home and then gone out again? It seemed highly unlikely. If he really was buying more beverages, what had he been doing for the rest of the day?

Davey had the music playing as instructed. He had placed a chair in the corner with his music case and his guitar next to him on a frame. Directly in front of the chair was the music stand. He had affixed the nameplate to the back of the stand with paper clips and had the small cards in a discreet pile at the edge of the stand. "Shall I start?" he asked Carla.

She smiled encouragingly. "Go for it."

She saw the first guests walking up the pathway and immediately went to summon the girls and Mrs. Young. Carla partially hid herself behind a half wall that separated the entry from the hallway. Mrs. Young was all joyous greetings and full smiles. The two girls looked professional. Davey began to play but then stopped. He re-tuned the strings, took a deep breath, and began again. *"Greensleeves,"* thought Carla. *Perfect.*

There were people coming in dribs and drabs for about ten minutes, and then the steady flow of guests began. That happy and chatty atmosphere that begins to signal the success of an event was slowly developing. Carla heard raucous laughter coming from the dining area. It suddenly struck her that not one single person had asked where Kenneth was.

Cecily remained by the entry while the last few guests sauntered in. One of the later arrivals was a man wearing a bright purple bow tie. It looked ridiculous. The woman accompanying him wore bright purple too. Presumably, that was the point, Cecily supposed. He murmured a thank you as he took the flute of and leered at Cecily rather lewdly.

"Hello, little lady …"

"Terence!" warned the purple woman, and he slinked off.

"Yuck," said Cecily quietly.

"Thank you, Cecily. If you would, please place the last few glasses on the table. Go through to the kitchen and have a quick drink of water or juice, please. You and Jeannie can start handing around the savouries in ten minutes." Carla went to see if she could find Glenda.

Glenda was ensconced in a corner with her sister, talking rather furtively. She saw Carla approach and took a sip of her wine.

"Glenda—and Marion isn't it? The place looks lovely. I was just wondering if you could fill me in about your father. Where did he say he was?"

"He didn't. He called me and said he was buying more stuff for drinks. There was a lot of background noise, and I couldn't hear too well. I thought he said something about racing cars, but he just wasn't making sense. I told Mother he had called to say he was buying more alcohol for the party, and she said he had better get a move on." Glenda took another sip of wine.

Jeannie was explaining to Cecily how to hold the large serving platters, high and to the side, steadied with one palm.

"Hey, that guy with the stupid bow tie. Sleazebag, eh?" remarked Cecily.

"Yes. I'm trying to make sure there's always someone else between me and him," Jeannie agreed. "The food looks pretty good, doesn't it?" Jeannie took a few swigs from the water bottle that Carla had supplied. Cecily followed suit.

"Your mum's done a brilliant job, I reckon. Apart from the purple-tied sleazebag, I'm having a good time myself!"

"Let's go, then!" They both picked up their platters and moved out into the crowd. Gradually they made their way around the room and found themselves close to the entry. Davey was putting back up music on prior to changing a guitar string.

"The music sounds great, Davey." Jeannie smiled encouragingly.

"Yeah, thanks. And look—the cards and everything. I wasn't expecting ... Two people have taken cards, and one of them asked if I gave guitar lessons ..."

The party conversation buzz was in full swing. Mrs. Young was flitting around, making sure she was talking to everybody.

"Excuse me," said a voice from the doorway. It had been left open to allow a through breeze. A man stood there looking pointedly at Davey and the girls. "Speedy Taxis. I have two passengers for this address, and they don't seem to have any money. I need forty bucks, please. I've got another fare waiting."

"Oh, right." Jeannie handed the platter to Davey and went off quickly to find Carla. Luckily, she was coming out of the kitchen. Jeannie whispered urgently into her ear.

Carla spied Mrs. Young talking animatedly to the purple couple and swiftly made her way across to them. "I'm so sorry to tear you away, Mrs. Young. I won't keep you a minute." Carla smiled apologetically at the couple, took Mrs. Young's elbow, and led her aside. Carla briefly explained that a taxi fare needed to be paid for two guests.

Mrs. Young looked completely confused. Her daughter Glenda joined them. "Is something wrong, Mother?" she asked.

"I need forty dollars," Maureen said without further explanation.

"It's for a taxi fare." Carla said bluntly.

Glenda looked around the room and spied her husband talking to a busty blonde. "Barry." She approached him with a lighthearted laugh. "Can I borrow you for a moment?"

He excused himself from the blonde and moved closer to his wife.

"I need forty dollars," she said without ceremony. "Quickly." Barry immediately took out his wallet and handed over a fifty-dollar note. Glenda virtually snatched it out of his hand and took it straight to Carla.

Assuming that she had been delegated to deal with it, Carla took the money straight to the taxi driver, who put it in his pocket. At that moment, a man and a woman stumbled through the doorway singing a raucous version of "Dancing on the Ceiling." They almost fell to the floor, but somehow managed to stay upright by wrapping their arms around each other and wilfully steadying themselves.

"Roma?" said Cecily.

"Cecily?" said Roma.

"Father?" said Glenda.

"Kenneth?" gasped Mrs. Young.

"Bloody hell!" said Barry as he watched Kenneth and Roma slowly and deliberately sink to the floor.

CHAPTER 19

Davey handed the tray back to Jeannie and had a go at bodily lifting up Mr. Young. Barry rushed to his aid. Glenda followed his lead and attempted the same thing with Roma. It took considerable effort, but eventually everyone was at least standing, if a bit wobbly. Carla joined them and indicated that they should transfer their charges through to the laundry at the back. It was a generous-sized room and the farthest away from everyone else. Maureen appeared to be transfixed to the spot until she saw them moving the drunken pair along.

"I did say we didn't need more alcohol, Kenneth. You shouldn't have worried." She looked around at her guests and then swept out in the general direction of the departing mob.

Carla instructed Jeannie and Cecily to continue with the finger food selection, and she herself picked up a tray of drinks from the table and joined them. Gradually conversations began again, and soon almost everyone had a beverage in one hand and something edible in the other. Breathing a sigh of relief, Carla returned her drinks tray to the table and made towards the laundry. Cecily followed her.

On reaching the laundry, Cecily handed her food platter to Davey and asked if he wouldn't mind taking her place for a few minutes. Davey was actually pleased to be out of there and decided that after one round of waiting on guests, he would get back to his guitar.

"Mrs. T," said Cecily to Carla, "they need eggs, bacon, and coffee."

"What?"

"Roma and him. They need eggs, bacon, and coffee."

"Do you *know* these people, Cecily?"

"Roma is my dad's girlfriend. I don't know why she's with him. But when she comes home to Dad the worse for wear, Dad always says she needs eggs, bacon, and coffee. It works, honest." She turned and returned to her post.

So many questions were whirring around Carla's head.

"Kenneth. Kenneth, who is this woman?" Mrs. Young was looking aghast at her husband. "Just what is going on?"

Kenneth grinned at her stupidly.

"Mrs. Young," Carla ventured, "is there any chance we could give them eggs, bacon, and coffee?" She was aware that she must sound totally off her trolley.

"Brilliant!" said Barry. "I've heard that. Something to do with the fat."

"Maureen, if you return to your guests, we'll … um … see to … the late arrivals."

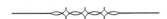

Barry, obviously familiar with the layout of the house, went through to the kitchen and proceeded to locate a frypan, plates, and cutlery. Glenda joined him and found eggs and bacon in the fridge. The two of them proved to be a tour de force. Glenda cooked, and Barry brewed strong coffee.

Carla asked the erring couple to move through to the kitchen as if they had booked a table in a restaurant and sat down opposite them just in case they should start wandering. Much to Carla's surprise, once the untimely breakfast was ready, they tucked in ravenously. Carla felt able to check on the party, and Mrs. Young.

Davey had taken his place in the musical corner once more. He was back to "Greensleeves," but that was of no matter. The girls were still smiling and the platters almost empty. The food had obviously been acceptable.

"You might have to wash those up in the laundry, Jeannie. We're ready for the sweets. The kitchen is rather crowded at the moment."

"Don't worry, Mum. We'll work it out."

Carla smiled gratefully at the two of them. It would seem there was more to Cecily than met the eye.

Lizzie was perched on a bar stool at Mary's breakfast bar with a glass of wine.

"Shall I lay the table, Nan?" asked Sarah.

"It's such a treat to have you here, Sarah. I don't expect you to work!"

"It beats assignments, and I know where everything is. Which tablecloth?"

"Oh, not a tablecloth. I bought a really nice beaded runner and table mat set today."

Sarah opened the door of the dresser. "These ones? They're lovely. Turquoise is beautiful, isn't it?"

Mary was finishing off the salad and had just popped the herb bread under the grill.

Mike and Jim were outside at the barbecue. Bill was adeptly turning lamb chops (a personal favourite) with a pair of sturdy tongs.

"Sarah seems to be going well. I've got a granddaughter to be most proud of."

"I won't disagree with you there!" Mike was wondering how he could steer the conversation towards Mary's concerns for Jim's perceived change of behaviour.

"Mike, I know we've deliberately avoided in-depth talks about … you know. The bad time …"

"No recriminations, Jim. We all make mistakes. We all make poor judgement calls."

"I know, I know." Jim went quiet.

"How's the world of books?" Mike had managed to secure Jim a job in a large bookstore through a friend who owed him a favour. It involved everything to do with the stock, organisation of the storeroom, placing orders, making deliveries, and so on. It was a far cry from the demands of finance; nonetheless, it suited Jim well.

"Good, good. People are still buying books, thank heaven. Son, I …" The patio door slid open. "We're ready when you are!" called Mary. "Righto."

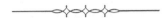

Hugh couldn't decide what to do with his Saturday night. Louis was at a friend's place. He could have gone too, but he was avoiding Dannii, who was bound to be there. She was all right, just loud and over the top about everything. Ben might be free. Thoughts of Ben led to thoughts of Jeannie. He felt bad about kissing her. For a start, he knew Davey liked Jeannie. He liked Jeannie himself, but he wasn't ready for any serious dating or anything. He wanted to get into college, qualify, and travel. He was going to have to tell Jeannie that. And he knew it would be awful. She lived next door, for God's sake. Louis's friend was only a couple of streets away. He might walk there after all.

Carla was using the large table in the laundry to lay out the sweet finger foods on the platters. Jeannie and Cecily were bringing the plastic boxes through from the kitchen. Carla asked them to cut the soft nougat into slices to be placed around the edge of a glass plate that would accompany the tea and coffee self -serve arrangement on the buffet. A glass bowl of malt chocolate balls that Carla had thrown in at the last minute went in the centre of the plate. Easy. Classy. Well done.

Cecily was full of admiration for Carla and Jeannie, and she was trying hard to make a good impression. She felt she was going OK until Roma turned up with what's-his-name. What the hell was that about? She struggled with Roma at the best of times. Selfish cow.

Jeannie was pleasantly surprised at how Cecily had been willing to do whatever she was asked, with no fuss. She had to find out more about the two drunks and how Cecily fitted in with them. It was all very odd. And Cecily's Dad—that was odd too. All concern on the phone but not driving her anywhere. Encouraging her to make the most of her opportunities yet shacking up with … well.

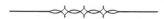

Glenda and Barry were whispering furtively in the corner of the kitchen.

"She—Roma—needs to be put it a taxi and sent home. Father needs to be taken upstairs and made presentable before Mother starts making any speeches. I mean, he can't possibly make any speeches, can he?"

"Another taxi?" said Barry. "Another fifty bucks?"

"This is an *emergency*, Barry."

"Bloody hell," he said, taking out his phone.

Between the two of them, Glenda and Marion managed to get Roma around to the front of the house in readiness for the taxi. She had been telling them what a lovely man Kenneth was and how he had been buying everyone drinks at the Rose and Crown. When they were thrown out, he had told Roma not to worry cos he knew where there was a great party happening. If that was it, though, she'd seen better dos at the RSL. The bacon and eggs were all right. A bit more coffee might have been nice, though.

"Alfred Gardens," Roma instructed the driver airily as she climbed into the back.

"Sixty dollars," said the driver by way of response.

Glenda rushed indoors to find Barry.

"Bloody hell," he said, opening his wallet.

Barry had managed to get three cups of strong coffee into Kenneth before taking him upstairs into the main bedroom in order to make him respectable. By this time, he was reasonably coherent but not at all happy.

"Just what has been going on here, Ken?" asked a bewildered Barry. Ken was normally so accommodating that it was almost nauseating.

"Where shall I start?" bemoaned Kenneth.

"At the beginning," said Barry as he opened the wardrobe doors and examined the contents on the hanging rail.

"I woke up really early and suddenly remembered that I had been moving everything around in the workshop. I'd switched the power off for the freezer and used that cord for the racetrack. It had been off since Thursday night."

Kenneth watched Barry lay out a fresh shirt and a suit on the bed beside him.

"I panicked. *Really* panicked. This bloody party has been all Maureen could think about or talk about for months." He removed his already loosened tie and began unbuttoning his stained shirt. "As soon as I opened the freezer door, I knew it was all ruined. I stopped thinking straight. I was trying to hide it all in bin bags. I thought maybe I could find a twenty-four seven store and buy enough stuff to replace it. I got dressed, left the house, and started driving around trying to find somewhere."

"Maybe a quick wash?" suggested Barry. Kenneth nodded in agreement.

Buttoning up the fresh shirt a few minutes later, Kenneth continued miserably.

"I couldn't find anywhere open, so I drove down to the beach to wait for a couple of hours." He snorted at himself. "Fell asleep. Can you believe it? Woke up in an even bigger panic."

Barry thought he looked exhausted. Probably only the coffee was keeping him awake.

"I drove around and found a deli, but I didn't have a clue what to buy. So I didn't buy anything. I ended up in the pub at lunchtime, had a drink or two, fully intending to phone Glenda and spill the beans, hoping she would come to the rescue."

"What about Roma?"

"She was in the bar. Started talking. I bought her some drinks and ended up buying drinks for everybody. By the time I phoned Glenda, I was as … paralytic … as the proverbial newt." He gave a hollow laugh. "So here I am, a pathetic disgrace and about to get the bollocking of my life from the woman that I have supposedly lived in domestic bliss with for forty years."

CHAPTER 20

"Thank you. Sorry we can't stay longer," Lizzie said, holding on to Mary's hand warmly.

"My fault, Nan," Sarah said, kissing her on the cheek. "I need an early night so that I can really and truly get my assignment finished tomorrow."

"Of course. We understand. It's been lovely—and I've used my new table setting!" Mary laughed.

Mike embraced his dad, sorry that there hadn't been an opportunity to really talk one-on-one. There were a couple of occasions when he felt Jim was trying to contrive some time for them to interact without it seeming dramatic, which of course was what Mike was doing also. All attempts on either side were unsuccessful, however. Each of them felt sure that something was definitely on the mind of the other.

Barry sat Kenneth down on one of the plush sofas, got him yet another cup of coffee from the buffet, and selected a few sweet treats to tempt him, which he balanced on the saucer, having placed it on a small coffee table adjacent to the sofa. Sitting down next to him, Barry attempted to engage his recovering patient in what would (hopefully) be interpreted by the guests as normal and rational conversation. He hadn't expected to be working quite so hard this evening.

Mrs. Young invited Carla upstairs to the main bedroom whilst she powdered her nose, making an excuse as to checking her thank-you list. As soon as she closed the bedroom door, the party hostess made for the edge of the bed and sank down onto it mournfully. She was fighting tears but seemed determined not to give way, probably fearing that she would not stop. Carla sat next to her but said nothing. She put one arm around her shoulder and gave her a gentle squeeze.

"Thank you, Carla. You've been marvellous. I just don't understand Kenneth at all. Today of all days."

"Do you know what I really think, Mrs. ... Maureen? I think Kenneth felt a little left out. Men often find solace in their sheds, don't they? And then he made that awful mistake with the powerpoint and, knowing how important this was to you, became really stressed. I mean *really* stressed." (Carla had been versed with a brief outline from Barry.) "None of his behaviour was deliberately bad. He just didn't know what to do or who to turn to."

"What on earth will my guests be thinking? Saying?"

"Don't worry about that. Look, how about we hand around another course of bubbly. Then, instead of your planned speech, you ask each of your daughters to highlight a couple of incidents from their growing up that involve you and Kenneth together. Then simply thank people for coming, thank them for the unnecessary gifts, remind them to sign the guest book, and ask Barry to propose a toast."

"If you think ..."

"You powder your nose and I'll send your daughters up here so you can put your heads together. Yes?"

Maureen nodded her assent and made for the en suite.

Jeannie and Cecily had positioned the celebratory cake centrally on the buffet, with the extra cupcakes plated on either side. They collected the final round of drinks from the kitchen and began circulating. By now, all the guests were laughing and chatting freely. There was even a couple sharing an amusing story with Kenneth. The couple took drinks from the tray. Kenneth demurred, preferring to stick with the coffee for now, thank you. Barry was no longer keeping guard, presumably because he felt the crisis was over.

The "purple creep," as Cecily called him, well inebriated by this stage of the proceedings, treated both Cecily and Jeannie to a particularly unsavoury leer whenever they passed by.

Davey was quickly selecting a Rod Sewart album that featured love ballads from the forties and fifties to give himself another brief break. Having drunk the entire contents of the water bottle supplied for him by Carla, he would just grab a glass of tap water from the kitchen and perhaps a bite to eat if there was anything left over. Barry was in the kitchen, opening and shutting drawers in search of something. He wasn't perturbed at all when Davey walked in.

"Don't suppose you've seen any matches. Or a lighter? I'm going a bit stir-crazy." He withdrew a pack of cigarettes from his jacket pocket by way of explanation. "Great music, by the way."

"Thanks. No, I haven't seen any. Have you tried the laundry?" All sorts of things were found in Davey's laundry at home.

They both exited the kitchen and crossed the hallway to the laundry. The door was closed, but they could hear muffled sounds coming from within. Barry opened the door to find a red-faced and angry Cecily pressing her back against the door of the linen press, brandishing a floor mop in front of her with two hands as if it were a pitchfork.

"Don't you even *think* of coming *anywhere* near me, you filthy old man," she spat vehemently.

In the middle of the room, the object of Cecily's ire stood with his arms raised as if involved in a bank heist. Lowering his hands on sight of Barry and Davey, he began coughing politely and fingering his purple bow tie with exaggerated correctness.

"Excuse me, gentlemen. I think there has been some kind of misunderstanding. I was in search of the bathroom," he slurred.

"Terence," said Barry. "How much have you had? You know where the bathroom is. Are you all right, luv?"

"I will be when he clears off. I was looking for tea towels, and he followed me in here. *Creep.*"

Terence made a hasty retreat.

"Sorry," said Barry. "Bit awkward. Kenneth's brother."

"Creep," Cecily reiterated.

"Bloody hell," said Barry. "Have you seen any matches? Or a lighter?"

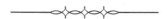

"I hope Davey's gone all right. I'd have given anything to be a fly on the wall." Greg and Helena had opted not to put the TV on after dinner.

"He's just embraced the whole thing with such maturity. I've been amazed."

"His outfit looked good too." Helena filled the kettle. "Thanks for doing that. I should've thought."

"You've had a lot to think about." Greg stood to get mugs and milk. Normally conversations were easy between them, but since the whole Betty thing started, there had been an awkwardness.

"Did you phone the agent?" asked Helena.

"I thought we were talking about Davey."

Helena looked up sharply. "What do you mean by that remark, Greg? I'm as thrilled with Davey as you are." She took the mugs from him and slammed them on the counter.

"Hey!" said Greg.

"I just wanted to know if you phoned the agent," she said as she spooned the coffee into the mugs, spilling some of it. She grabbed a kitchen sponge and wiped up the mess. The kettle boiled.

"And I wanted to talk about Davey," he said, adding the water and milk.

"We can talk about Davey. We can talk about Hugh and Louis as well. Did you phone the agent?" Helena turned deliberately and looked him in the face. "Well?" she waited.

"Yes, I phoned the agent." He sat down with his coffee.

"And ..." prompted Helena.

"And I refused the offer." Greg sipped his coffee. It was hot, but he didn't react.

"Yet you didn't tell me?"

Greg looked at her, stood up with his coffee, slowly walked out of the room, and closed the door. Helena heard the TV go on.

Both daughters suggested that the host couple should be seated side by side on the sofa. Glenda and Marion stood by the cake. They shared a couple of innocuous little anecdotes about family life when they were young and then handed over to Barry.

"Ladies and gentlemen," Barry broached confidently. "We all know to whom we owe thanks for this wonderful party, thrown in honour of Maureen and Kenneth and their achievement of forty years together."

Hoots, cheers, and murmurs of congratulation circulated through the gathering.

"Maureen never does anything by halves, does she? Unforgettable, Maureen."

Maureen smiled gratefully as if at her adoring fans.

"But bear with me. There's something else I want to show you. Please make sure your glasses are charged and then be so good as to follow me."

Some confusion arose as Barry strode purposefully out of the house through the back door and on around towards the workshop. Carla, Davey, Jeannie, and Cecily had been in the kitchen beginning the clear-up when they heard the sounds of mass exodus and couldn't resist finding out what was going on. Both roller doors were fully open, and the space was emblazoned with every available light. The workshop almost accommodated the crowd, apart from the tardy few who remained outside.

Barry mounted an upturned plastic crate and waited for quiet.

"Ladies and gentlemen …" He gestured expansively towards the racetrack that stretched along the full side of one wall, looped, and then came back again. "You see before you evidence of the loving care and dedication shown by a grandfather for his grandsons. Kenneth has worked tirelessly to make this crowning event happen tonight!"

Kenneth's two grandsons, both aged twelve, stood at the starting line of the track, each armed with a control monitor. On the track, ready to race, were two cars, one red and one green.

Barry winked at the two boys. "Are you ready, boys?" He raised a chequered flag. "I present to you"—Barry was obviously in his element—"the inaugural race of the Young workshop racetrack!" He decisively brought down the flag, and the race began. The boys demonstrated surprising skill as they steered the remote cars around the track to the finish line. Huge roars erupted as the cars broke the line almost simultaneously.

Barry raised his glass. "Ladies and gentlemen, I give you Kenneth and Maureen!" Both grandsons approached their grandparents and handed them a control monitor each.

"Come on, girlie!" said Kenneth, dragging Maureen towards the track. "Let your hair down!"

CHAPTER 21

"Well done, everybody. One thing that party didn't lack was a touch of drama!"

Carla's car was full of chat on the way home.

"Your playing was great, Davey. Would you do it again, do you think?" Carla was pleased that her gut feeling was right.

"Oh, man. I'd jump at the chance. Someone asked if I gave lessons. They took a card."

"Barry was amazing, wasn't he? He turned the whole thing around. Thank you, Cecily, for the egg and bacon advice." Carla thought it might not be advisable to ask how she knew of the cure. Perhaps she wouldn't mention Roma either.

"It's all right. Thanks, Mrs. T, you know, for the job. It was good … 'cept for that sleazebag."

"So you're none the wiser about Jim?" said Lizzie as she made them all a final drink for the night.

"No. I'm sure there's something worrying him. I guess I'll just have to wait until he's ready to talk."

"Sarah was a bit quiet too, I thought. I suppose it could be the assignment playing on her mind; but … I don't know … She didn't quite seem herself … Well, not relaxed, anyway."

"Do you think we worry about other people too much, Liz?"

Lizzie laughed heartily. "Impossible. We're hard-hearted lawyers, remember!"

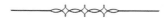

Douglas heard Ben enter the house via the garage. "Hi, Dad. Mum not back yet? Did you get the gen about the missing husband and everything?"

"I heard some, and your mum was worried about it all panning out in the end. 'Course, your mum's born for this kind of thing, isn't she? Don't stand in the corner too long or you'll get the dickens organised out of you! But the misper in this case is rather critical. Anyway, as I said to her, 'You've done all you can do. In the end, if people don't want to come to the party ...'" They both roared with laughter at the unintentional joke. "Quite literally, as it happens!"

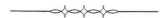

"Are you sure you don't want me to come in and talk to your dad, Cecily?" asked Carla. After receiving the rundown on the laundry incident, Carla was horrified." I really feel as if I should. I'm responsible for you; you were in my care."

"You couldn't know. And anyway, nothing happened. He was scared of me in the end."

"Well, make sure you tell your dad about it and I'll come and talk to him if he wants me to, OK? Thank you for your hard work."

Carla watched Cecily knock, just to ensure that she was home and safe. A light went on, but there was a delay in opening the door. Eventually, it opened rather awkwardly. Carla was taken aback when she realised the man letting Cecily in was seated in a wheelchair. He waved, presumably by way of thanks to Carla, and closed the door.

"Goodness," said Jeannie. "I had no idea."

"Me neither," Davey echoed. "Poor man."

Poor Cecily, thought Carla.

Hugh and Louis came home together. The walk was just over a kilometre and well lit. Louis was well pleased with himself, as he had been a hit with the lovely Dannii. She laughed at almost everything he said. She had also taken a friend along, Tamsin. Tamsin also appeared to be quite impressed with Louis but was even more enamoured with Hugh. Hugh played a few games of pool, but for the most part couldn't really be bothered. He was going to have to tell Jeannie that the kiss was a big mistake. He liked girls. He liked Jeannie—she was lovely—but he just didn't want to go beyond friendship. How could he have been so stupid?

"Davey'll be home soon. S'pose he was brilliant."

"Louis, don't. It takes a lot of guts to play a musical instrument in public. He's really talented, and he's our brother."

Louis pulled a small twig of greenery from a shrub as he passed by and began shredding the leaves with his fingers. "Yeah, I know."

"Anyway, you did all right tonight—Dannii boy!" Louis didn't get it, but he laughed all the same. They punched each other lightly on the arm a few times and then raced the last few hundred metres home.

The program that Greg had been watching finished. Helena hadn't joined him. He'd hoped his point had been made, but to be honest, Helena wasn't seeing anybody's point just now. He'd run everything through in his head several times. In fact, this problem took up most of his headspace most of the time. There was Betty's need of care. The three boys were growing up, but the stability and the security of a good home base was still essential; he'd be damned if he was going to allow them to be robbed of it. He and Helena were continually at odds. There had to be a solution, one that didn't involve the sale of the house and a mass relocation to Betty's place. The thought of it horrified him. He could just take control and insist on having his own way, but that could be even more horrific. He could lose Helena.

"Hi, Mum."

Davey had returned. Greg switched off the TV and went through to the kitchen. Davey was glowing.

"Sooo ... tell us ... How was it?"

Brimming over with the events of the evening, Davey had obviously enjoyed the musical opportunity immensely, yet he was keen to relate the stories he had been part of. Helena was seated at the table, listening intently to Davey's experiences. Greg remained standing, leaning against the dresser. He was pleased for Davey and realised that his youngest son, often somewhat isolated, had considered himself part of a team. It was most gratifying.

"Dad, do you think I could ... you know ... do this?"

"You mean for a living?" asked Greg.

"What I *do* know," interjected Helena before Greg could answer, "is that you're probably exhausted and now isn't the time for discussing future careers. It's great that it all went so well, honey. Shall I make you cocoa?"

Greg bit his tongue. What was wrong with her, for goodness' sake? It was a case of *Who are you and what the hell have you done with my wife?*

Likewise, Carla and Jeannie were giving Douglas the rundown of the night's events. In hindsight, it was all quite hilarious. Douglas made them all hot milk, claiming they needed something to help them sleep because they were both hyper.

"I'm a bit concerned about the sleazebag, though. He probably should be reported, don't you think?"

"Well, it's tricky when nothing did actually happen. What would we report him for? He could say he was threatened by a manic girl brandishing a broomstick!"

"Cecily knows how to look after herself, but somebody else might not," Jeannie added.

"Maybe I could find out from Mrs. Young if there have been problems before. I might leave it until Monday, when I take her the bill. I don't know how shocked she'll be at the final cost, mind you!"

Climbing into bed, Jeannie allowed her thoughts to wander into Hugh territory. He had kissed her—actually kissed her. When he took her hand and twirled her in towards him, her whole being tingled. She was sure he was going to kiss her, and then he actually did. As tired as she was, it took ages for her to drift off to sleep, despite the hot milk, because she relived the moment repeatedly. Sometimes the scene replayed itself in another setting: centre stage, with an entranced audience watching on. Or on a film set, where their costumes changed partway through. Or alone on a ballroom floor, she dressed in white and he in a tuxedo, guests seated around magnificently decorated tables, smiling at them indulgently.

In the morning, she awoke slowly, and then wondered how Hugh would go about asking her on their first date. He would probably ask today. Jeannie was in heaven.

CHAPTER 22

Hugh woke early and immediately consulted his favourite online site detailing events that were on locally. He found a dog show, a fashion swap meet, and an amateur one-day volleyball tournament being held at the courts behind the GetFit gym. It was a promotional event for the health club. Anyone could turn up and be slotted into a team for the day. Knockout games would be played, but an allocation of points following each game meant that the teams played throughout the whole event and were competitive until the end. Excellent. He hoped that he could persuade Louis and Davey to join him and the three of them would be out all day. He couldn't face Jeannie yet. He would talk to her tonight.

Greg and Helena were each aware of the other being awake, although they lay back-to-back without touching.

"Shall I run us a bath?" Greg ventured tentatively.

"A *bath*. OK. Lots of bubbles. There's a bottle in the vanity."

Greg made his way to their bathroom, plugged the bath, turned on the taps, and located the bubble mixture. It promised an unsurpassed sensory experience for one's skin, along with an indulgence of aromatic fragrance formulated to ensure the totality of bodily well-being. *Keep it neutral*, he warned himself. *Don't talk about the house. Don't talk about*

Betty. And maybe not the boys. Greg kept the water running until the bath was over half full and the bubbles were rising above the rim.

"I'm in," he called out, sinking into the hot water.

Helena had stripped off before coming into the room and stepped in gingerly, then slowly sat down opposite him. "Nice," she said.

Greg recalled their first meeting. A mutual friend had invited both of them to a student union–run rally operating under the banner of Youth for World Change. Neither of them was a student nor particularly enamoured with the idea of lobbying parliament from the steps leading up to the city war memorial. Both, however, had recently broken free from half-hearted relationships. Greg had caught out his girlfriend snogging the guy behind the bar at the back of the pub. Helena had dumped Peter unceremoniously when she discovered him rifling through the pockets of her jacket when he thought she was in the loo. Once introduced to each other by their friend, some kind of magical interchange took place between them. They had never looked back, proving themselves strong in character and relationship. Until now. Greg's heart was aching with the strain of trying to close the chasm widening between them. He and the boys were on one side, and Helena was on the other.

Jeannie didn't delay in showering and dressing. She wanted to appear presentable but not ready enough to go out. It took several attempts for her to feel satisfied with the way she looked. Opting in the end for cut-off shorts and a tie-dyed tee, black flats, and her hair pulled back in a ponytail, she checked in the mirror and decided that the result was satisfactory. Cute and casual.

Of course, she had to find herself something to do. She couldn't sit around in her bedroom waiting for Hugh to call and ask her out. It was difficult to set her mind to anything, though. She tried reading—there was a book she needed to finish for English by Tuesday—but the words swam about on the page. She should eat some breakfast, but she couldn't face it. Perhaps the red flats would be better. She reopened the wardrobe doors. Actually, she could tidy the wardrobe. Reorganise. Chuck out the stuff she didn't really like anymore.

Carla rapped on the door. "I'm making scrambled eggs!" she called.

"OK, you first. Best part of your week," Greg said as he used his hands to gently splash water over his shoulders.

"No. You first."

Greg took his time. "This is pretty good."

They both heard the unmistakable sound of the shower in the main bathroom being turned on and the accompaniment of the three boys sharing the space.

"They must all be going out together. I like it when they do that."

"Your turn," Greg prompted. "Best part of your week."

Helena sighed. "Mum telling me I could come home for the week. But that's the worst bit as well because …"

"Because what?"

Helena cupped some of the soothing water in her hands and splashed it on her face. She rubbed and rubbed as if she wanted to erase her features. "Because you're not bloody there, are you? The boys aren't there either. I have to go back and *you're not there*."

Greg took her hands and held them. He knew he had to remain calm. "No. We're not there. But, Helena, listen to me. I really don't think you need to be there either."

Helena stood up abruptly, splashing water everywhere. "Of course I have to be there!" she yelled. She stood still, just looking at him and then at the mess on the floor. "Mum can't be on her own, can she?"

Hanging on to the edge of the bath, she almost tumbled out and on to the bath mat. She steadied herself and grabbed a towel, which she wrapped around her torso roughly. She stared accusingly at Greg.

"These are the facts, Greg. Mum isn't well enough to be on her own day and night. We don't have room for her here, and anyway, uprooting her would be unfair. She lent us the deposit for this house, and she's helped us out with money more than once. *We owe her.* She has a big house that would accommodate us. When we sell this one, we can add a granny flat to hers—and that's our duty done. Everybody is happy." She stormed out.

Greg stood and climbed out of the bath. He removed a towel from the rail and began drying off. "No, actually. I strongly disagree."

"Disagree with what?" Helena countered irritably. She was behind with the washing and had to go with undies she didn't much like from the back of the drawer.

"That everybody is happy. I would say, in fact, that nobody is happy."

"Well," said Helena quietly, "you can't always get what you want."

Hugh, Louis, and Davey could bike ride to the tournament easily. They ate cereal, filled water bottles, and slapped some sandwiches together. Davey was keeping them amused with his anecdotes about the party. He could be a fair mimic when he chose to be.

All three of them were well versed in the compilation of the necessary requirements for a day out on the bikes: hats, water, food, sunscreen, money, and so on. They could pack stuff into their backpacks efficiently whilst conducting quite in-depth updates on the lives of anyone they found interesting. Between them, there were plenty of friends and acquaintances, not to mention a healthy supply of idiots who had gotten involved in something completely stupid and were good for a laugh.

"Wait until you hear about the lovely Dannii!" Hugh goaded.

Louis reddened and squirmed, but secretly he was pleased about the raise in estimation with regard to his reputation.

Davey was determined not to let on to Hugh that he had seen the kiss. He would put on a brave face at the tournament.

Hugh tore a large scrap from the almost-empty cereal box and found a marker in the cup that held pencils and pens. "Davey, can you check the bathroom looks OK? Louis, can you just rinse those dishes?" He scrawled a note on the cardboard letting Greg and Helena know that they were all out for the day. Finally, he packed the cereal boxes and bread packages away and wiped down the table. By the time Helena had dressed and made her way to the kitchen, they were gone.

"Sorry, Mum, but I just can't eat any more." Jeannie felt quite nauseated when she was faced with a plate of scrambled eggs on toast. She threw the remains of her breakfast into the bin and loaded up the dishwasher with her dishes and all those still languishing in the sink. Adding the cube of detergent to its designated zone, she adjusted the dial and turned it on.

"You love scrambled eggs!" Carla responded. "I hope you're not sickening for something. Oh, give Josie a call this morning, please. Check she is on the mend."

"I'll go round and see her!" she chirped. Fantastic. The wardrobe could wait. She needed to talk to someone about Hugh or she would burst. She'd make sure she was back early in the afternoon. It might not be a bad thing if he called in the morning and was told she was out.

"A visit might be better left until the afternoon, don't you think? If it was an allergic reaction, then every few hours would make a difference. Why not ring this morning and see how she sounds?"

Jeannie was trying to come up with a plausible reason for going to Josie's as soon as possible.

"You look nice, by the way. Out to impress someone?" Carla joked.

"No, course not. I just remembered that I had this top—and I like it." Jeannie fiddled with her ponytail self-consciously.

"Are you OK, love? You're probably tired from yesterday. Why don't you go back to bed for a while?"

CHAPTER 23

"Jim!" said Mike. "This is an unexpected pleasure!" It struck Mike as ironic that it was becoming usual for his father to behave oddly. He couldn't remember the last time Jim had turned up on his doorstep unannounced. It wasn't that Mike minded; it was just another example of Jim's current out-of-character behaviour.

"Anything wrong?" Mike stepped back from the doorway and indicated that Jim should come in.

"No, no. It's a beautiful day. Could we take a walk?"

"A walk? Yes, I suppose we could. I might pick up a paper. I'll just let Lizzie know." Mike was pleased to find Lizzie in the garden. "Jim has asked me to go for a walk. I said I'd get a paper."

"Well, it's a nice day for a walk." Mike loved the way they could communicate almost via a form of code, allowing them to understand each other without overtly stating facts.

"Hello, Jeannie. How did the big do go?" asked Josie's mum.

"It went well, and Mum was very pleased, but there were some hilarious moments. I thought I could come around and cheer Josie up a bit."

"That's a lovely thought, Jeannie. Josie's been left with a really sore throat. I sent her back to bed for the rest of the morning. She would love to see you this afternoon, I'm sure."

Jeannie said she would call later, related the conversation to Carla, and threw herself onto her bed in frustration. If she didn't talk to someone soon, she'd go mental. Her mind was doing somersaults. The open wardrobe doors beckoned. She took everything out and threw it onto the floor, right down to the last squashed tissue and stray panty liner.

First remove all the obvious crap, she advised herself. She located an empty BuyMart bag to contain the rubbish. As well as the debris that somehow lodges itself into the corners and at the back of the shelves, she threw away knickers with worn elastic and bras now too small. She'd need a few more outfits suitable for dating; most of her stuff was a bit "cutesie" or practical and boring. She sorted and hung items. Definitely room for improvement. She had some money in her allowance, and she was due her wages from the party. Mum usually boosted her coffers when she needed some clothes.

Sarah found Lizzie in the garden, tidying up a small flower bed.

"Shall I make us a pot of coffee, Mum? Gosh, it's a beautiful day, isn't it? Where's Dad?"

Lizzie laughed. Sarah was so … fresh. You knew exactly where you stood with her, and she rarely had an unkind word to say about anybody.

"A pot of coffee would be lovely. Yes, it is a beautiful day. And your Dad has gone for a walk with Jim."

"A walk with Jim? Ah."

"Ah? Did you know Grandad was coming around?"

"No. The garden looks nice. Are they freesias?"

"Yes, I'm nearly done here. If you can wait for two minutes, I'll come in with you and we can make coffee together. Have you got a lot of your assignment still to get through?"

Mike was running through scenarios in his mind as Jim was talking about a program he had watched on TV recently. It was all to do with the effects of sport sponsorship on lifestyle, apparently. He wouldn't have come to Mike's house to talk about a TV program. What was going on with him? Mike felt he was correct in ruling out the womanising angle. Equally, he was sure it wasn't a gambling problem. Could he be sick? Or could Mary be sick? He seemed too upbeat for that. Maybe he should just ask him straight out.

"Anyway," said Jim as they reached the forecourt of the service station where Mike would buy the paper, "that wasn't what I wanted to talk to you about."

For pity's sake. Was he doing this on purpose or what?

Jeannie's morning dragged on, and her spirits dragged with it. Eventually, she offered her assistance to Carla.

"Actually, I thought a roast would be nice tonight. Could you check I've got enough veggies and pop down to Fresh Goods for anything I'm short of—potatoes, carrots, pumpkin, and green beans? Then I can concentrate on the accounts."

"Sure," she said half-heartedly.

"I think your dad might offer to cook tonight." Carla expected a response, but there was none, leaving her to wonder again if Jeannie was coming down with a bug.

Carla had spent a lot of time on the account that was to go to the Youngs for their ruby wedding anniversary party. The bill was much larger than originally expected, due to the amount of extra tasks that had to be undertaken to carry the whole thing off as smoothly as possible. She was compassionate to a degree, but she was essentially a businesswoman. Yet she obviously wanted more work to come from this, so it was a matter of striking that balance between charging for a legitimate service and exercising good customer relations. Itemising everything was important, ensuring the Youngs realised how much had been done to cover the unforeseen circumstances—of which there were many, Carla mused.

Carla would list the visitors' book and pens as complimentary; they had been surprisingly inexpensive anyway. Ben would be paid for purchasing and installing the lights; however, the discretely itemised workshop clean-up at one hour at no charge indicated goodwill. Of course, the finger foods had to be included, but apart from a collection charge that covered fuel, Carla detailed them as being cost price only.

Intending to deliver the bill in person on the pretext of concern for their welfare, Carla was having second thoughts regarding the wisdom of the timing. If she were to call in later this afternoon, albeit a Sunday, rather than waiting until Monday, Kenneth would almost certainly be there (suitably mortified, one would think). Possibly his wife would be as well, and she might play on the sympathy angle.

Lizzie was listening to Sarah enthusiastically outline the content of her assignment. Its broad title was "Australia, Remote Communities and Distance Education." The essay topic was as follows: *Discuss the effective implementation of distance education in remote communities and its role in the academic and social development of individual students, their families, and the wider context of global understanding.*

"You know, Mum, I'm thinking it could be brilliant to spend a year tutoring on a remote property. We had someone come and talk to us who did it for three years. You become part of the family, help out on the property, and play a vital role in the education of those particular children in a much broader sense rather than simply in the classroom."

The two of them were sharing coffee. They heard the two men coming around to the back entrance of the house. "I can't wait to tell Lizzie." That was Jim's voice. Lizzie frowned; Sarah took a sip of her coffee. Virtually bursting through the door, Jim and Mike stood facing Sarah and her mum. Jim was grinning from ear to ear.

"Is there any more coffee?" Mike asked.

"Freshly made," announced Lizzie. "Tell me what?"

Jim took his time pulling out a seat from the table, sitting himself comfortably, and adopting the attitude of the chairman of the board. "I have some good news."

Lizzie waited; Sarah took another sip of her coffee and avoided her mother's eyes.

"I …" began Jim slowly and deliberately. "That is, Mary and I are going on a little holiday." Jim looked at Lizzie intently.

"Lovely. Margaret River?" she asked, knowing of their fondness for the place. They would occasionally treat themselves to an overnight stay. They had friends who owned a caravan kept permanently on site.

"No." Jim allowed a broad grin to spread across his face. He thanked Mike for the coffee as it was placed in front of him.

"We, Mary and I, are going to … Europe!"

"Europe?" Lizzie gasped. Sarah took another sip of coffee. Lizzie just stopped herself in time from blurting out, "How on earth can you afford to go to Europe?"

"I've been saving up ever since, you know, our circumstances changed. Mary has never been one to regale me with recriminations. She has just been there, managing economically, making sacrifices. She deserves a decent holiday. And I mean one where she doesn't have to lift a finger. So I've saved a small amount regularly, hoping to surprise her."

Lizzie thought he must be able to walk on water if he'd managed to save enough for the two of them to go to Europe. You didn't go to Europe for a weekend mini-break.

"And …" Jim grinned again. He was obviously enjoying this. "I've bought a scratchie from the newsagency every week without fail. Never won a cent. Until three weeks ago. Three weeks ago, I won …" He paused for dramatic effect. "I won twelve thousand dollars!"

"What?" Lizzie spilled her coffee. "Shit. Sorry. Twelve thousand dollars?"

"Yes. With that and what I've saved, not to mention Sarah's help. She went with me to the travel agency a couple of times to get me a good deal and work out the best value for our money. We have enough for flights and a coach tour for fourteen days, seeing the sights and sounds of France and Italy. Mary doesn't know yet. Now that I've spoken to Mike, I can tell her. I've had a tough time keeping it a secret."

"Well, I'm almost speechless. I'm thrilled, Jim. Really. I think you should finish your coffee and get home to Mary. Go break the news before the strain becomes too much!"

CHAPTER 24

Douglas did indeed offer to do a roast dinner, leaving Carla free for the afternoon. The Young's bill needed to be dealt with personally. Their house wasn't a great distance from Josie's, so Jeannie could visit her then. On their way home, they would take Cecily's wages to her and, Carla hoped, talk to her father about the issue with the purple creep, as both girls referred to the guilty party.

Jeannie was quiet on the way to Josie's place. She had been quite hyper in the morning. It could be just tiredness. That party had probably been the most demanding job Jeannie had ever done. In fact, it was the most demanding job Carla had undertaken. Did she want more of the same—the ongoing planning, the last-minute stresses, the vagaries of unpredictable clients? To be honest with herself, she thrived on it. This is what she had been working towards. All the small jobs were great, for they kept the wheels turning, but the challenge of an event was something else entirely.

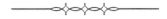

"Why don't we make the most of the boys being out and find a movie each on FreeFlicks?" Helena suggested to Greg. She felt bad about losing her temper in the bath. "Sorry about this morning. I don't know what got into me."

Greg had hardly uttered a word since the argument. Helena was turning into someone else, and he felt powerless to stop it. Maybe he was turning into someone else. They had always been convinced that they were rock solid. Strong. Unbreakable. Perhaps it was merely a pipe dream.

"OK," Greg said. "Are we going for old or new? Classic or crass?"

"You decide. I don't mind. I'll get tea and biscuits. Or would you prefer popcorn?"

"Whatever." Greg turned on the necessary devices and began scrolling through the menu. "Whatever you like."

Josie looked better than she had at school, but she was still unwell. Her throat was sore. Jeannie had to do most of the talking. It hardly seemed appropriate to share her news about Hugh, so she gave a rundown on the events of the party, which served to cheer them both up. There was plenty of time for Hugh to ask her out, wasn't there? He'd probably call in tonight.

"Tell you what, Josie. Seriously. I reckon Cecily is quite nice. She worked hard at the party and got cornered by this real creep in the laundry, so she grabbed a broom or mop or something and threatened to spear him with it if he came an inch closer! He soon cleared off. And when we dropped her home, her dad answered the door in a wheelchair. She hasn't got it easy, and when you look at what we've got …"

"She could do with a friend, right?" Josie croaked.

"Maybe two?"

It was around three o'clock when Carla drew up on the driveway of the Young's house. She calmed herself for a few seconds before ascending the tastefully decorated steps leading to the front door. She rang the bell.

"Carla, how lovely. Come in." Maureen was casually dressed but fully made up. The house looked immaculate.

"Goodness," said Carla. "You've done well! Have you got seven efficient dwarves hidden away somewhere?"

Maureen declined to answer.

"Forgive me for calling on a Sunday. I had to drop my daughter off to visit a sick friend, and I wanted to check everything was …"

"Carla, I have to thank you for everything you and your staff did yesterday to make sure our special party ran smoothly."

Carla wondered if Maureen might be suffering from selective amnesia. "Ran smoothly" hardly fitted the bill.

"Kenneth is in his workshop, and I know he wants to express his thanks personally. I'll go get him for you." She glided out of the room with almost royal aplomb, leaving Carla to admire the array of gifts and cards arranged on the buffet.

Kenneth soon appeared—without his wife. He excused Maureen, saying she was in the garden picking some fresh flowers. "Please do sit down." He waited for her to be seated and then sat opposite her, smiling disconcertingly.

"I wouldn't blame you, Carla, if you thought my behaviour from yesterday appalling and unforgivable. To a degree, I feel that myself." Noticing Carla's discomfort, he said, "Please just hear me out." Silently he gazed out of the window for a moment. "I *am* sorry for causing stress and worry to the people involved in my … absence. I'm *not* sorry that I got drunk. I've only been drunk twice in my life, and the first time around it was due to my brother. He kept spiking my drinks, and I had no idea. No. I have been so pathetically compliant all my adult life. I'm sick to death of myself, frankly. Getting drunk and behaving badly meant that people did actually *see* me. *I* saw me. And it's no good blaming anybody else for my being considered … lily-livered." He nodded backwards as if to indicate his wife in the garden. "I chose the easy way out every time. Well, no more. I shall give my opinion and let my preferences be known."

Kenneth held out his hand towards Carla. "The invoice, I suppose?" He took the envelope and opened it. Scanning it briefly, he said, "Oh, yes, I think that's very reasonable in the circumstances. If you would be so good as to wait here, I shall write a cheque immediately."

Carla was astounded. He returned quite quickly with a cheque, which Carla thanked him for.

"Oh, Mr. Young, there is one more thing. Your brother. He was at the party ... wearing a purple bow tie?"

"I believe so, yes."

"He behaved inappropriately towards one of my young female staff ..."

"Oh, heavens. He's such a ridiculous man. He thinks he's still *got it*, as it were. In truth, he never really had it! I would be very surprised if he caused any harm. He would turn tail and run at the merest hint of reprimand. What did you want to do about it?"

"Well, if he could be spoken to so that he is aware that we know what he is up to ... Perhaps a police officer would be able to remonstrate with him?"

"Would you be willing to leave it with me? Believe it or not, I think Barry might well be able to put the fear of God into him for us. Might that suffice?"

"From my experience of Barry, Mr. Young, I think he might just prove to be the perfect candidate for the job!"

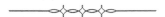

Cecily answered the door to Carla and Jeannie. Instead of asking them into the house, Cecily stepped outside and pulled the door almost closed. Carla handed Cecily the envelope with her pay inside.

"Thanks, Mrs. T."

Carla wasn't sure about the *Mrs. T* tag, but she wasn't going to address that issue now.

"May we step inside, Cecily? I was hoping to speak to your dad."

"Yeah. Sure. Go through."

The place looked reasonably clean and tidy. It was quite sparsely furnished, however. Enough space had to be allowed for a wheelchair,

Carla presumed. Mr. Reid sat on one side of a small table. He was in the middle of a card game—with none other than Roma.

"Hello, dear!" said Roma." Fancy seein' you so soon!"

Jeannie was once again amused to see her mother momentarily stuck for words.

"Yes … um … Roma. I was hoping to have a word with Mr. Reid." Carla looked directly at Roma, who gave no indication of understanding that some privacy might be in order.

"Could you give us a moment, Ro?" asked Cecily's dad.

Roma collected the cards together, thereby closing the game, took a bit of time to sort them into a pack, placed them in the centre of the table, and sniffed her way out of the room.

"Thank you, Mr. Reid. I just wanted to advise you that the incident involving Cecily has, I believe, been dealt with. The fellow in question has now been advised by several people, within his family and without, that should any further incidents give cause for concern, he will be reported to the police. I have made an official note in my work diary of the incident should Cecily, or yourself, feel it necessary to take the matter further."

Mr. Reid nodded. "Cecily told me about it. She knows how to stand up for herself. You all right with that, Cecily?"

"Yeah. Thanks Mrs. T. Stupid Creep." She smiled.

"Cecily worked well, Mr. Reid. I hope to be able to employ her again. I'm sorry," she added, looking at her watch. "I must go. I'm running a little late. I apologise for taking up some of your Sunday afternoon."

Outside, Cecily apologised for Roma. "She stays for about a month and then choofs off. Says she needs a break. Then she just turns up again. But Dad seems to like having her around."

Carla didn't quite know what to say.

"Enjoy spending your money, Cecily." Jeannie touched her arm lightly. "See you tomorrow."

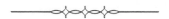

Fortuitously, it was in between movies that the landline interrupted the rolling credits of *Mama Mia*. Greg picked up the phone.

"Betty," he said after a brief interlude. He continued to listen as Betty filled him in on her reason for calling. "OK, then. Sounds good. I'll let Helena know. Have a good time. Take care and remember we are only a phone call away."

Helena looked at him expectantly.

"Betty is going to Marinda's place for a week. She said she hopes you don't mind having another week off."

"Oh." Helena used the controls to exit *Mama Mia*. "I'll start on the jacket potatoes while you find *The Terminator*, OK?"

"Sure," replied Greg.

Helena waited for him to look up and smile at her. But he didn't.

CHAPTER 25

Hugh, Louis, and Davey spilled around the corner of Capstan Court, raced each other to the driveway, and slowed as they rode into the garage at around five o'clock. Greg had moved the bike rack to the rear of the garage and had just finished clearing off two tiers that made up part of a shelving unit that stood against the wall.

"Boys, I've cleared off these two shelves for you to put anything related to bike riding on, rather than having stuff scattered around everywhere. How was the tournament?"

Storing their bikes and paraphernalia away, they related the events of the day. Because they had gotten there early, they had the pick of the teams and had opted to all be on the same side. The purpose, of course, was to annihilate all of the opposition and declare themselves the champion team by the end of the day. They had almost made it. Entering the final round with the top score, they battled their opponents neck and neck until the final five minutes, when, according to Louis, fatigue set in. Moreover, the umpire made two crappy decisions. They ended up in second place.

Greg relished these occasions when the three of them demonstrated brotherly affection. Raising kids was bloody hard work. Seeing them interact so positively was gratifying. It strengthened his resolve. He would somehow make Helena see it. He had to.

"What did you and Mum do?" Hugh asked

"Movie marathon."

"Let's guess," Davey mooted. "Mum's was … *Notting Hill*. No, *Mama Mia*."

"Too clever by half." Greg grinned. "You won't guess mine."

"*Thomas the Tank Engine?*" Louis said, completely straight-faced.

Greg picked up an oily rag and threw it at him. "How many times?" asked Greg. "*Percy* is my favourite. Get in the shower, you lot, before I …" He picked up another soiled scrap and threw it in their general direction. "Before I lose my rag!"

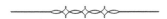

"All done. Hopefully. I've got to check it and do a final edit, but right now I need a break. What can I do?" Sarah crossed to the stove, where Lizzie was stirring a Bolognaise sauce. "Yum."

"You can get the angel hair, if you like. The water is almost boiled." Lizzie used a teaspoon to taste the sauce and smacked her lips with satisfaction.

Mike came through with a bottle of red and made his way toward the glass cabinet. "Are you joining us in a glass, Sarah?"

"I think I just might. After all, assignment achieved."

"I still can't believe you kept that secret, you know? You're terrible at keeping secrets. Well, you have been up until now, that is!"

"I can't believe it either," Sarah said opening the pack of pasta. "There were a few tricky moments. Carla saw me in town when I was meeting Grandad at the travel agency. I just denied it was me … and she swallowed it. And it was a double whammy, really. There was the holiday secret and the fact that Grandad won all that money. I can't believe *he* kept that secret. From you and Nan."

Mike continued with the explanation. "The reason for the botched attempts at revelation to me was, of course, the battle with his conscience over using that money for what he saw as selfish reasons. He wondered if I'd feel resentful. As if!"

Lizzie stopped stirring, turned off the flame, and put a lid on the saucepan. She crossed to Mike, put her arms around his neck, and kissed him. "I love you, Mike Mitchell," she said, picking up her wineglass and taking a generous gulp.

"Here's to family," said Mike, raising his glass. "Especially ours."

Helena had hoped that after the second movie finished, she and Greg would be able to talk properly. She had only half watched the movies, knowing them practically by heart anyway. Her mind had been taken up with her senses and feelings, which, frankly, were torn to shreds. Rather like victims of The Terminator, she thought wryly. As soon as the movie finished, Greg went out to the garage on the pretext, she was sure, of needing to reorganise something or the other.

Deciding that she would find something to reorganise herself, Helena settled on the area they used as a study. A shelf fixed to the wall at head height held boxes of photographs. Rather ashamed of the gathered dust that she had neglected to attend to prior to house viewings, she reached up to get them down from the shelf. The phone rang abruptly, startling her. She dropped all three boxes. "Dammit," she said as she went to answer the phone. It was the real estate agency.

"Helena. Great news. That young couple who made an offer? They love the house so much that they are prepared to pay the asking price— subject to finance. What do you say?"

"Wonderful." She fiddled with the phone cradle. "Greg isn't here at the moment." (Half lie.) "He'll be thrilled." (Lie.) "I'll get him to call you. Thanks. It's … wonderful." (Complete and utter bullshit.)

Helena returned to the upset boxes of spilled photographs. She had been meaning, of course, to make up beautiful albums, dated and documented, with designer-edged frames and filigree borders. There was something so honest about the photographs just being housed in boxes, though. They recorded simple moments rather than special occasions.

There was a photo, probably taken by Betty, of them on the day they moved in. Odd bits of furniture and cardboard cartons surrounded them. Photos of each of the boys in her arms when they came home from the hospital. Birthdays, silly outfits, and dress-up days. New bikes and remote-control cars. She picked them up slowly and deliberately and placed them back in the boxes in no particular order. Their lives to date. Precious and irreplaceable. And the common factor? The house. The home that they had created over twenty years. She cried. The tears of happiness she shed as she looked through the photographs turned into tears of sadness when she placed the boxes back on the shelf.

What was she thinking? How could she leave? Why was she forcing everyone into this? Greg was right. This wasn't the way to keep everyone happy. Not even Betty. She heard the boys enter through the back door and make for the shower. She rubbed the tears away and ran her fingers through her hair.

"Did I hear the phone?" asked Greg as he walked into the room. He looked at Helena's face. "What? What is it?"

Helena walked across to the shelf once again, took down the photograph boxes, and laid them on the desk.

"Look," she said as she removed the lids. "Look at us." They both picked up a small handful of photos and sifted through them. They laughed together at the missing teeth and the ice cream–covered faces. They groaned at the ill-advised haircuts and embarrassing fashion choices.

"Greg, I don't know what to say, except that I am so, so, sorry. We can't, can we? We can't leave. This place is so much a part of who we are." The tears began again, and Greg took her in his arms. "I've just felt so guilty for wanting to hang on to it so badly at the expense of Mum, who didn't have what I have. But she made it possible for us to have it."

"She did what she did out of love for us. You don't need to feel guilty about anything. Anything at all."

"But we can't just leave her to cope on her own …"

"I know, I know. There will be another solution. We just don't know what yet."

Louis walked into the kitchen draped in a towel. Finding the room empty, he moved into the sitting room. "I'm starving. Are we eating soon …? Or am I interrupting?" He grinned.

"About twenty minutes. Go get dressed, please!"

"The only thing I haven't done is pay Davey. Would you like to take his money around?" Carla and Jeannie were stacking the last few things in the dishwasher; Ben and Douglas were washing and drying the pots and pans.

"That might be a bit awkward," Jeannie said.

"You haven't had a falling out with Davey, have you?"

"No. Of course not."

"How about we both go, then? I want Davey to have his money, and I want someone else to hear how well he coped with the evening."

Jeannie hesitated. She really wanted Hugh to come to see her. How would it look if she went there? This was getting complicated. "OK," she said.

Carla gave a rapid yet firm knock. Hearing the chatter from within, she surmised that everyone was home. Opening the door part-way, she called out, "Hello, Brownes! May I come in?"

Jeannie's insides were going haywire. She needed to calm herself. A few moments spent breathing deeply should settle her down a bit. She hung back rather self-consciously.

"Come on down!" said a cheerful Greg. "Don't mind the mess." Greg was revelling in Helena's about-face as well as their all being together for their communal jacket potato feast on Sunday night. Carla went in ahead of Jeannie.

"We shan't keep you long. I'm sure you would like to have your money, Davey?" Carla handed over an envelope. He took it tentatively and thanked her.

"Thank *you*, Davey. You did a first-class job. As well as providing some great *ambiance*." Carla grinned. You proved so supportive under some trying circumstances! Have you told everyone?"

"Oh, we've heard all about it," said Helena. "What a turn-up, eh?" She almost felt delirious with relief after admitting to Greg that she was wrong. If His Holiness the Pope had walked in and requested a beer and a fag, she'd have found them somewhere and sat him down in front of the TV with an episode of *Totally Tasteless Tattoos* and a meat pie.

Jeannie had overcome her nerves enough to join everybody. She was standing behind Carla. Her eyes met with Hugh's as soon as she walked in. He returned her gaze briefly, looked away quickly, and left the room.

Jeannie turned and ran out through the open door. The chatter came to a halt, and everyone stood still. The only sounds were those of Jeannie's rapid footsteps and forlorn sobs.

Carla ran after Jeannie, Greg followed Hugh, and Helena looked at Davey, giving a confused shrug of the shoulders.

Davey put the envelope in his pocket. "Hugh kissed her," he said. For him at least, that explained everything.

CHAPTER 26

"My course will finish in a few months. I could stay at home for another year, keep working for Mum, and get one more qualification under my belt." Ben and Douglas were chatting amiably following the clean-up after dinner.

"But ...?" prompted Douglas.

"Well, I guess qualifications are always good, but this kind of job requires skills that are learnt hands-on. The more experience I have, the better landscape gardener I'll be. I could approach one of the small garden companies, but I don't want to get bogged down with mowing lawns twenty-four seven."

"Could you keep working for Mum, get your extra qualification, and begin branching out on your own as well? It's a lot at once, I know, but if you want to have your own business, you have to start somewhere, and you have to be prepared to put in extra hours and do what is necessary to keep your head above water as far as earning a living goes."

"I hear you." Ben filled the kettle. "But I don't know that I can really start a business from this house. You don't want your garden being turned into a nursery ..."

They were interrupted by Jeannie bursting through the door and running straight to her room, sobbing as she went. The unmistakable sound of moaning bedsprings indicated that she had thrown herself on her bed.

Alarmed, they both approached her room, but she swiftly got up from the bed, slammed the door shut, and yelled at them, "Leave me alone!"

Hugh made for his room. Greg followed him swiftly, walking in behind him and closing the door. Hugh sat down on the bed, and Greg sat beside him.

"What was that about?" Greg waited patiently for an answer.

"I've done something really stupid."

Greg didn't speak.

"I kissed Jeannie. Accidently."

"Accidently?"

"Well, not accidently, really. I meant to kiss her, but I shouldn't have."

"Go on."

"I like Jeannie. She's lovely. And we had fun working together on the cards for Davey. I guess I worked out that she really liked me, and I … kissed her."

"OK. That doesn't really explain what just happened, though, does it?"

"As soon as I got home, I knew I shouldn't have done it. For one thing, Davey's crazy for her, but I'm not ready for a girlfriend. I want to finish school, get to uni, and qualify. Then I want to travel. I really want to travel. I'm pretty sure she was expecting me to ask her out. You know—do the whole dating thing. I can't. I like her, but I can't."

"Don't get annoyed, but I have to know: it was a kiss and nothing else, right?"

Hugh looked up smartly. "Dad!"

"OK. Sorry." *Thank God for that,* he thought. "Well, you just have to tell her. Just like you've told me."

"I really can't."

"You must, I'm afraid. And quite soon."

A far from calm Carla rushed into the kitchen with an enquiring look at Ben and Douglas.

"Jeannie?" They both pointed in the direction of her room.

"What on earth?" Douglas asked.

Carla said nothing. She stood still for a moment, took a breath, and then went and stood outside Jeannie's bedroom door. She knocked gently.

"Go away."

"Jeannie, please let me in."

"Leave me alone."

"I'll just sit with you. Please let me in."

"Go away!"

"More than anything else, it's embarrassment," Douglas almost whispered to Carla as they got ready for bed.

"But she's not talking. I just want to talk to her."

"She will. Give her a bit of space."

They had all tried, even Ben, although he hadn't a clue what he would say if she did let him in. Hugh came around—but not for long because she wouldn't talk to him either. Carla had tried to fill them in, but she wasn't clear herself what was going on. One minute she was paying Davey and complimenting him on a job well done, and the next moment everything had turned to tears. Quite literally.

The moment Douglas saw Hugh, he realised that there was something amiss between the two of them. Aware that Hugh was in possession of that disarming quality that combines brains with diffidence (which women seem to find irresistible), on top of good looks, it was not in the least bit surprising that Jeannie should fall for him big time. It was almost inevitable, in fact. Probably because they had all noticed Davey's attraction to Jeannie over the last six months or so, they had not considered such a turn of events. He felt it wise not to say any of this to Carla, however.

Greg informed the three boys that from now on, they would have a morning lift with Helena to school but would have to catch the bus home. That way, should Helena want to call on Betty at any time during the week, she was free to do so. In addition, they were making their own lunches. If they forgot or ran out of time, they could either go hungry or use the canteen at their own expense. Greg was actually quite surprised at the lack of objection.

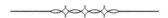

"Oh God, Greg, I forgot." Helena was slipping into Greg's favourite night-time tee of hers, which stated, "Yes, it's all for you." She continued. "The real estate company phoned. That couple you wouldn't accept an offer from have come back with the asking price, subject to finance. What shall we do? I feel bad letting them down now."

"Nothing is agreed; nothing is signed. They'll get over it. How about we wait to see if they get financing? Then we're not the bad guys!"

Knowing that Hugh had been unable to speak to Jeannie, Greg sought him out early the next morning.

"I'll try to see Jeannie tonight," Hugh said. "I've behaved badly, I know."

"No, actually," said Greg, "you've behaved impulsively. There's a difference."

Carla was pleased to see Jeannie eat breakfast dressed in her uniform, hair done, the works. There was, however, a barrier around her. She obviously was in no mood to talk about anything related to Hugh. Perhaps a full day at school and talking to Josie would somehow ...

All the platitudes were ready in Carla's head: "You're both young." "If it's meant to be ..." "True love never runs smoothly." "If you really love someone, let them go." Etcetera, etcetera, etcetera. Crap. When someone you love is truly hurting, you just want to take the pain away.

Jeannie was sitting alone on one of the benches close to the art room. She was sorting out her bag, tidying it as she went through it, throwing away any bits of unwanted paper or rubbish and putting them in the bin. She was looking for the sketch she had done of the old building nearby that housed the local library, intending to submit it for the bimonthly school magazine.

"No Josie today, then?" It was Cecily.

"No. Her mum must have thought she needed an extra day, poor thing. Cecily, may I ask …? You don't have to tell me …"

"About my dad and the wheelchair?" Cecily sat down beside Jeannie and picked at her nails. They were bright purple, which was against the rules. Strictly neutral was the order of the day. She might get away with it until lunchtime.

"It's been me and Dad for a long time. As I said, he's OK, my dad. It's better when Roma isn't there. But he gets lonely, you know?"

Jeannie held off searching for her sketch and listened intently.

"Anyway, Dad was in a car crash about six months ago. We had to find a place that could take a wheelchair and didn't have high rent. It'll be better when he can drive, but he has to have, you know, changes—*modifications*—to the car. He's trying for a grant, but it will take ages."

Jeannie found the sketch.

"That's really good," said Cecily.

"I'm really sorry about your dad. Thanks for telling me."

"Yeah. Bummer. Dad says that now he's in a wheelchair, he knows that he's always lived in a wheelchair. Too scared to get out there and do stuff. That's why he wants me to make the most of my opportunities." Cecily studied her purple nails. "You know what, Jeannie?" Cecily looked away at the wall of the undercroft emblazoned with positive slogans painted by Year 11 students a few years ago. She focussed on one that urged anyone willing to take the time to decipher the graffiti-styled artwork to climb to the peak one step at a time.

"What?" Jeannie prompted.

"You. With your family. You could be anything you fuckin' well wanted to be. Anything. 'Scuse the fuckin' language." She smiled, and Jeannie smiled back. Cecily admired her nails again.

"How long till they make me take this stuff off?"

Dressing carefully in cut-off jeans and a crop top, Jeannie kept an unobtrusive lookout for the boys next door coming home. To her surprise, she noticed all three of them walking together at the head of Capstan Court. They must have caught the bus. She gave them about twenty minutes and then walked around to their front door.

"Oh … Hi, Jeannie." Louis hesitated, not sure whether to invite her in or not.

"Hi, Louis. I was wondering if Hugh was home." Hugh appeared behind Louis, and Louis made a rather hasty retreat.

"Hugh." Jeannie smiled. "Can you spare me five minutes?"

"Sure," he said, stepping aside as if to ask her in.

"I thought we could just walk and talk. I shan't keep you long."

"Oh, fine." Nonplussed, Hugh called out to his brothers that he would be back in a few minutes and then pulled the door closed.

"Shall we walk to the swings in the park?" Jeannie suggested. There was a walkway to a small play area where the children often played when they were little. It featured three swings and an elephant slide.

"I suppose you heard about all the party mishaps from Davey," Jeannie began, and filled up the space between them with descriptions of the Young family. It didn't take long to reach the swings. Jeannie sat down on one, and Hugh, rather than sit next to her, took the one on the end of the row.

"Jeannie …" Hugh faltered.

"Hugh," Jeannie interrupted. "I'm sorry, but I must ask you to hear me out. The thing is, to put it bluntly, I can't go out with you. On a date or anything. I'm really sorry if your feelings have been hurt in any way, but I have to be honest. I'm just not ready for the whole girlfriend/boyfriend thing, you see? Josie and I are saving for a holiday the year we finish school. I want to do some travelling, see the world a bit. So I'd rather we just stayed friends."

Hugh was dumbstruck.

"Please say it's OK." She smiled appealingly.

"Yes. It's OK. Travel is … good." He could hardly believe what he had heard.

"Friends, then?"

"Sure," Hugh said, feeling far from sure.

"Great." Jeannie checked her watch. "Oh, I must go. I should phone Josie; she's been quite unwell."

"You go, then," said Hugh, and he sat and watched her cute little self hurry off down the pathway.

Power to you, Jeannie, she thought to herself. *All power to you.*

CHAPTER 27

G reg was checking his monthly report before packing up to go home. He was presenting it to the management board the next day. The hospital didn't suffer from a lack of income, the medical staff were experienced, the support staff well trained, and the staff relationships, in general, rather good. The problem they did have, Greg mused, was mathematical in nature. The surrounding area had grown exponentially over the last five years. The doctor-to-patient ratio wasn't good, simply because the need for either an extensive expansion of the campus or an additional hospital in another suburb, whilst acknowledged as necessary, hadn't come about, despite election promises and protests by way of newspaper reports declaring that there was no room at the inpatients or that patients lost patience with bed shortages. The resultant shortfall sometimes led to complaints implying ineffective service or even negligence. Greg found that a personal call from him immediately prior to any surgical procedures, explaining any limitations brought about by cutbacks or budgetary constraints, worked wonders.

"Greg Browne speaking." He didn't get work-related calls on his mobile, and being a little distracted by the document he was reading, he took no notice of the caller identification.

"Mr. Browne ... Greg, if I may. Harry Charles, from Charles's Real Estate. I have the most exciting news for you! Presumably, you and your wife have discussed the young couple who are crazy about the house, desperately trying to get financing. Well, earlier today, I received a further enquiry from interstate. I explained the situation to them, and they were bitterly disappointed. They haven't viewed it, of course, other than on the Internet, so it's all speculative, but all indications are that they are willing to outdo the current offer by several thousand!"

The line fell silent. "Mr. Browne? It seems you did the right thing by sticking to your guns."

"Yes." Dammit. Helena had come right around to his way of thinking. Now there were two offers on the house, both of which exceeded their expectations. They hadn't thought of a satisfactory solution for Betty. This was likely to muddy the waters and take them back to where they started.

"That is great news. I'll ... er ... speak to Helena tonight. Thanks."

"I wondered where you'd got to!" Carla had been sorting laundry and putting away bedding and towels. "I didn't hear you go out." Jeannie actually looked positively perky, Carla was pleased to note. She said nothing further, hoping that Jeannie would fill her in about whatever it was that had transpired between her and Hugh.

"Oh, I just walked to the park and back. Hey, you know how Josie and I have been saving for a holiday once school has finished? I've been thinking. A trip to Bali or whatever might be nice, but it's a bit, you know, ordinary. It would be cool to see if we could get into a university in another place, interstate or even abroad. I think you can exchange if you get really good marks. What do you think?"

"I think that's a marvellous idea! What brought this on?"

"Oooh, I don't know. Let's call it girl power. I've realised that my future—what I make of it—is mostly up to me. What's that song you used to sing a lot? I haven't heard it in a while ... Jeannie began singing.

Don't even think, don't even try
to fetter me.
I am flyin' high.

Carla joined in:

*And the wide blue sky reminds me
Why.*

They hugged without speaking. They were on the same page.
"I am so, so proud of you, Jeannie."
"How can I help with dinner?"

Helena appreciated the extra time Greg had blessed her with by insisting the boys should catch the bus home. It felt a little odd, though. She made herself a coffee and took it back to her desk, deciding to phone Betty to check that everything was all right. Betty seemed completely rejuvenated, at least on the phone.

"Still here?" Gina noted. The office was quiet, so Gina pulled out a chair and sat next to Helena. "How is everything?"

"That's actually difficult to answer. Mum is currently staying with a friend, which takes so much pressure off, but of course that's temporary. We're not really any closer to coming up with a workable solution."

"So often, we women think we should *have* all the answers and also *be* the answer, don't we? You know, even the most satisfactory solution to a problem tends to have its drawbacks. Don't feel guilty about considering yourself and your own needs." Gina laughed. "My grandmother always used to say 'Whenever one is facing a problem, one should buy a new hat'! I never understood that, of course, but I do often find myself drawn to the shoe store when I'm stressed or worried. That colour looks nice on you, by the way." Gina stood and restored the chair to its allocated spot. "Forgive me, please. I've a thousand emails to check. You take care."

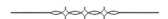

Hugh's mind was buzzing. It was odd, but he could hardly concentrate on anything at school. Exams were coming up soon, and he needed good marks to be offered a placement, but revision alone wasn't enough. He needed an edge. He needed work experience. As soon as he was home, he had a quick shower and set about making himself look presentable.

"Hot date?" asked Davey.

"Nope. Job hunting. You've inspired me with your gig!"

"Are you trying out at the mall?"

"Yep. Good a place as any to start."

"Mind if I come too? I've had a bit of an idea myself."

"I'm leaving in five minutes."

Greg arrived home shortly after Helena.

"I stopped off at Digson's to get ingredients for a curry," she said.

"Great," said Greg. "Shall we make it together?"

"I was hoping you'd say that. I had to guess at the ingredients." Helena filled the kettle.

"We'll see what transpires, then!"

Louis loped in, opened the larder door, and stood there as if expecting a request for him to place an order. "I'm hungry."

"Well, we shan't be eating for a while. Make yourself a sandwich or eat some fruit," Helena said as she opened the fridge door in search of milk. Louis reached in front of her, pulled out the vegetable drawer at the base of the fridge, and took out an apple. He loped out again, presumably returning to his video game.

"I'm sort of pleased he chose to eat a piece of fruit, but I know darn well he's too lazy to make a sandwich!" Helena commented good-naturedly. In truth, she was thrilled that everyone was behaving normally. "I wonder where the other two are."

Greg removed the teabags and placed the two cups on the table. "I ... er ... heard from the agency today ..."

Hugh and Davey chained up their bikes in the racks outside the mall and agreed to meet up again in about half an hour. There were two pharmacies in proximity of the shopping precinct. One was located within the mall itself, with an outside entrance and exit to allow for out of hours service to customers. It was a busy pharmacy, open from seven until eleven, seven days a week. The main entrance was closest to him, but he realised on entering that this must be a particularly hectic time of the day. The place seemed full of harassed mothers, tired children, fretful babies, and adults looking as if they were ready to collapse into bed any moment. Then there were people filling out scripts, a group of girls selecting make-up, someone trying out a sling to support a damaged arm, and one couple selecting reading glasses. It appeared chaotic. *Not the best time to enquire after a job,* Hugh thought. Maybe he'd try the other pharmacy. It was situated between a doctor's surgery and a professional medical centre housing a dental practice and an optometrist.

Hugh went into the pharmacy and was greeted by a smiling chemist. The gentleman was middle-aged. His smile revealed a mouthful of braces, and his eyes, creased in welcome, were partially obscured behind very thick glasses. The irony wasn't lost on Hugh. On answering Hugh's enquiry, it became evident that he was in possession of a heavy accent.

"No, no. Sorlee. Next door. He good help."

"Next door?" enquired Hugh, a little confused.

The man nodded and pointed in the direction of the optical store. "He good help."

Hugh thanked him and was about to return to the mall when he thought he'd call in to the optometrist, seeing as only a single customer was completing a transaction before leaving the store.

The man, who in fact looked like the gentleman in the chemist, minus the thick glasses and braces, offered a brisk, "Good afternoon."

"I'm sorry if I've made a mistake. The gentleman next door directed me to you … I think. I'm looking for some part-time work."

Davey made his way to the management office. A woman sitting behind a computer screen greeted him rather half-heartedly. Davey stated his purpose.

"You'll need a form," she said, retrieving a pad of blue A4 sheets from a drawer to her left. "Fill this out and return it. It'll be about seven working days before you hear anything. I don't make the decisions. It's up to the management supervisor. She handed Davey the form and then looked up at him properly. "I know you from somewhere."

"Um, I don't think—"

"Were you playing guitar at a party recently? Yes. My neighbours'. That turned out to be a right ding-dong, didn't it? Your guitar playing was the best bit!" She pointed at the form. "Put down as much information as you can. I might put in a word."

CHAPTER 28

Hugh telephoned the real estate agent the next morning. It was fortuitous that there had been two offers because it gave them some extra time. Helena hadn't hesitated when Greg told her about the interest from interstate. They weren't selling. It just wasn't an option for them. But something had to be done for Betty, and she had to be made to see that it was a case of making the best of things.

They had come up with two options: First, considering that Betty wasn't short of money, they could investigate the possibility of delivered meals, house cleaning, and gardening, with the two neighbours continuing to keep a check on her mobility-wise. The drawback: money doesn't last forever and neither does the goodwill of neighbours. Second, Betty could sell her house. Greg and Helena would forgo any of its worth and find Betty a nice aged care facility. Surely they did exist. The drawback: Betty loved her house as much as they loved theirs. It might set her back emotionally.

Upon Betty's return, serious discussions would have to be undertaken. Helena was dreading it.

Helena comforted herself by cooking up spaghetti bolognaise. It was easy to make, the boys loved it, and it somehow got everybody talking around the dinner table—although the talkfest had truly gotten going the previous evening (with the exception of Louis, who was apparently waiting on a call from the lovely Dannii).

They had both been impressed with Hugh, having taken it upon himself to look for a part-time job and coming home with the news that he was to be employed on Thursday nights and Saturdays. It had transpired that the optometrist he had approached was the brother of the chemist with rudimentary English language skills, having recently immigrated. He was a good chemist but obviously not yet able to converse satisfactorily with customers. Hugh was to help generally and liaise with clients. And Davey—quiet, introverted Davey—had enquired about the possibility of busking. Who'd have thought?

Louis returned from putting the bin out, at Greg's request, with the post in one hand. He dumped the small pile of correspondence on the dresser.

"What's in that yellow envelope?" Helena wondered aloud. "It doesn't look like a bill."

Louis shrugged but picked it up. "Dunno. A letter, I s'pose. Who sends letters? Haven't they heard of emails?" He handed the letter to Helena.

"I don't recognise the writing. Oh, I'll open it after dinner. Louis will faint with hunger soon."

At breakfast the following morning, Greg retrieved the yellow envelope from the dresser. "This envelope is addressed to you. Very neat hand too. Aren't you intrigued?"

"Oh, I'd forgotten all about that. Do you want to open it?" Helena asked as she fetched the cereal boxes from the crowded shelf in the pantry and placed them on the table. She took out two cartons of milk from the fridge, as one was almost empty, and watched as Greg opened the envelope.

Greg immediately scanned to the bottom of the page to identify its author. "Oh, it's from Betty."

Helena dropped the cartons onto the table, fortunately without spilling any milk, and snatched the letter from Greg's hand. "From Betty? Why write when she can phone? She's probably disowning us."

"My darling girl," she began. "I don't know if that's good or bad." Helena sank into one of the dining chairs.

> *My darling girl,*
>
> *You'll be surprised, I know. You won't recognise the writing. I'm dictating to Marinda. I don't think this predicament we find ourselves in is anyone's fault. Let's make that clear from the outset. We all want what's best for everybody, don't we? Because we are all caring people.*
>
> *The fact is, I understand that it will be difficult, and gradually become more so, for me to remain living alone. I don't want to be a burden—of course you would understand that. Even relying on neighbours too heavily doesn't sit well with me. I could sell up and probably find somewhere where I'm taken care of. But I really love this house. Apart from you, it was the best thing to come out of those years with your father. Bless his soul. I absolutely do not think you should even consider coming to live here with me. I can't quite think how that came about anyway. But I do know that it wasn't working.*
>
> *So, what to do?*
>
> *Marinda and I have decided to pool our resources. She likes the idea of coming back to the city for a while at least and knows plenty of people who would gladly rent her property. Our combined income will mean that we can employ people to do whatever we are unable (or unwilling) to take on. We have run all this past Jean too, who might even consider joining us. She has a dog—that can't be bad for security, can it?*
>
> *We plan on trialling our house share for one month and, if it runs smoothly, extend it to six months and then a year. (Us all remaining in reasonable health, that is!)*

My darling girl, I'm not even going to ask if this meets with your approval. It's what I want to do, and I want you to indulge me.

Your ever-loving mum
XXXX

Greg took the letter from Helena's hand and read it himself. The boys all burst into the kitchen at the same time. Collecting bowls and spoons, the three of them made for the same cereal packet and knocked over the open milk carton.

"Oops," said Louis, with no hint of apology.

"Not my fault!" Davey quickly grabbed the cereal box.

"Tosser!" laughed Hugh.

"Don't use that word!" Helena and Greg chorused.

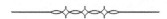

The following Saturday, Greg called on Mike and then Douglas to ask if they wouldn't mind helping him out with something before their regular game of golf. Hugh, Louis, and Davey stood proudly in the front garden of their house, a For Sale sign lying on the lawn beside them.

"I need to get this sign back to the agent," explained Greg. "Can you give me a hand?"

"Glad to, mate," said Mike.

"I've got a better idea," said Douglas. "Hang on." He went inside. He came out a short time later with Ben in tow. "Ben will take it back for you. How about that?"

The sign was soon dismantled and loaded into the ute that Ben used as a work vehicle.

"Are they expecting you?" asked Mike.

"I phoned first thing. In fact, I may have woken him up. Not a happy chappie! All drinks on me!"

They clambered into the car. Greg turned the music on and then upped the volume. The voice of Freddie Mercury said it all:

We are the champions.
We are the champions.
No time for losers 'cause we are the champions
Of the world!

Ben backed out first, with one leg of the For Sale sign resting unceremoniously on the edge of the ute tray. Greg's hatchback followed in its wake, allowing the trio of homes to settle once more into the familiar mooring they all knew, at Capstan Court.